How to Write a Bestselling Contemporary Romance

The Art of Swoon: Mastering the Contemporary Romance Genre

Just Bae

Contents

Introduction

As you embark on the journey of writing contemporary romance, you are engaging in a dialogue not just with your readers, but with the very essence of our contemporary world. This genre, fluid and ever-evolving, offers a unique opportunity to reflect on the zeitgeist of our times through the lens of romance. Your role as an author extends beyond storyteller; you become an observer, a commentator, and a visionary, weaving narratives that resonate with the immediacy of today's experiences, aspirations, and challenges.

In contemporary romance, you have the liberty to explore a broad spectrum of themes and settings, from the bustling energy of urban landscapes to the quiet charm of small-town life. Each setting provides a rich backdrop against which the drama of love unfolds, allowing you to paint vivid pictures of the places where modern romances bloom. The authenticity of these settings, grounded in your keen observations and research, adds depth and relatability to your stories, inviting readers into worlds that feel both familiar and enchantingly new.

The characters you create are the heart and soul of your narratives. In contemporary romance, these characters must navigate the complexities of modern relationships, embodying the diversity of human experience. Your protagonists can challenge societal norms, confront personal demons, and celebrate triumphs that speak to a wide audience. Through your characters, you have the power to champion inclusivity, representing a range of genders, sexual orientations, ethnicities, and life experiences. This not only enriches your stories but also ensures that your work resonates with a broader audience, offering windows into lives both similar to and different from one's own.

Moreover, contemporary romance allows for an exploration of current social issues and themes, from the impact of technology on relationships to the nuances of consent, mental health, and the quest for identity and belonging. These themes add layers of depth to your romance narratives, challenging you as an author to balance the light-hearted with the profound, the romantic with the realistic. Your ability to navigate these complexities with sensitivity and insight can turn a simple love story into a powerful commentary on contemporary life.

The dialogue you craft between characters is another vital element of contemporary romance. It must sparkle with authenticity, capturing the rhythms and nuances of real conversation while advancing the emotional and narrative arcs of your story. The incorporation of modern forms of communication—texts, emails, social media—into your dialogue offers dynamic ways to develop character and plot, reflecting the ways technology shapes our interactions and relationships.

As a contemporary romance author, you also face the challenge of keeping your narratives fresh and engaging amidst a wealth of tropes and conventions. Your creativity in reimagining classic scenarios, tropes, and dynamics can set your work apart, offering readers new perspectives on the themes of love, conflict, and resolution. This innovative approach not only captivates your audience but also pushes the boundaries of the genre, contributing to its growth and vitality.

Writing contemporary romance is, ultimately, an act of passion and courage. It requires you to pour your heart into creating stories that entertain, enlighten, and inspire. As you craft these narratives, remember that your voice is unique, your perspective invaluable. The stories you tell today become part of the fabric of contemporary romance, shaping the genre for future generations of readers and writers.

Welcome to the vibrant, challenging, and rewarding world of contemporary romance writing. Here, your stories have the power to touch hearts, provoke thought, and perhaps even change the way we see love in the modern world. Embrace this opportunity with both hands, and let your journey begin.

Preface

As a new or experienced author, you are tasked with crafting narratives that not only entertain but also reflect the complex realities of modern life. This genre, set against the backdrop of the present day, offers a canvas on which to explore the trials, triumphs, and intricacies of love with authenticity and depth.

Capturing Modern Love: Contemporary romance is distinguished by its setting in the modern world, a place teeming with challenges and changes that shape how we experience love. Your stories are windows into this world, offering insights into how people meet, connect, and navigate the obstacles to love in a time defined by rapid technological advancements, shifting cultural norms, and evolving societal expectations. The essence of contemporary romance lies in its ability to mirror these dynamics, making the genre not only relevant but deeply engaging for readers.

Reflecting Realism and Relatability: The strength of contemporary romance stems from its realism. Your characters live in the same world as your readers, dealing with issues like dating apps, career pressures, and complex family dynamics. This relatability is key to crafting compelling stories. Your readers should see parts of themselves in your characters and their journeys, fostering a deeper connection to the narrative. Authenticity in character development, setting, and dialogue ensures that your stories resonate, offering both escapism and reflection.

Embracing Diversity: Today's contemporary romance embraces a wide spectrum of experiences and identities, reflecting the diversity of the real world. As an author, you have the opportunity—and responsibility—to include a range of voices and perspectives in your work. This not only broadens the appeal of your stories but also enriches the genre as a whole. Diversity in contemporary romance includes exploring different cultures, sexual orientations, and life experiences, ensuring that every reader can find stories that speak to them.

Navigating Contemporary Issues: The backdrop of contemporary romance allows for the exploration of current social issues and themes. From the impact of social media on relationships to the challenges of mental health, contemporary romance can tackle topics that are both timely and timeless. As an author, how you weave these themes into your narratives can add layers of complexity and relevance to your stories, making them not just tales of love but reflections on the human condition.

Innovating Within the Genre: While contemporary romance may be grounded in the present, it is not limited by it. The genre is ripe for innovation, allowing you to experiment with narrative structures, points of view, and genre-blending elements. The essence of contemporary romance is fluid, evolving with the times and with the creativity of its authors. By staying attuned to current trends and listening to the diverse voices of your audience, you can push the boundaries of the genre, offering new and exciting perspectives on love and romance.

Prologue

The evolution of the contemporary romance genre is a fascinating journey through cultural shifts, literary trends, and the expanding horizons of love stories. This progression reflects not just the changing tastes of readers but also the broader societal transformations that influence what people seek in their romantic escapes. Let's briefly delve into this rich history, highlighting key milestones, influential authors, and landmark novels that have shaped contemporary romance into the vibrant and diverse genre it is today.

The Early Days: Post-War Romance and the Rise of the Modern Novel

The roots of contemporary romance can be traced back to the post-World War II era, where the genre began to distinguish itself from its historical and gothic predecessors. In these early days, authors like Mary Stewart and Georgette

Heyer laid the groundwork with their romantic suspense and romantic novels set in the times contemporary to them, albeit these settings are now considered historical by today's standards. These stories introduced readers to romance entwined with the social and cultural issues of their time, setting the stage for future exploration of more complex themes.

The 1970s and 1980s: The Boom of the Romance Novel

The 1970s and 1980s witnessed a significant boom in the romance genre, with the rise of mass-market publishing making books more accessible to a wider audience. It was during this period that the contemporary romance genre began to take a more defined shape, with authors like Danielle Steel and Nora Roberts emerging as giants. Their novels, often set in glamorous or everyday settings, spoke to the dreams and realities of their readers, combining passionate love stories with relatable characters and settings. Nora Roberts, in particular, has been a pivotal figure in the genre, her prolific output and ability to blend romance with elements of suspense and the supernatural setting a new standard for versatility and depth in story-telling.

The 1990s: Diversification and the Supermarket Romance

The 1990s saw the diversification of contemporary romance, with the genre expanding to include a wider range of themes, settings, and characters. This period marked the rise of "supermarket romances" - paperbacks readily available in grocery stores and accessible to a broad audience. Publishers like Harlequin and Silhouette dominated this space, producing series that catered to specific interests and fantasies. This era also saw the emergence of romantic comedies and chick lit, sub-genres that offered lighter, often humorous takes on love and relationships, exemplified by authors like Helen Fielding with "Bridget Jones's Diary," a novel that blended humor, romance, and the trials of modern womanhood.

The 2000s to Today: The Digital Revolution and Genre Blending

The advent of the digital age and the rise of self-publishing have dramatically transformed contemporary romance since the 2000s. The ease of publishing and distribution has led to an explosion of diversity in the genre, both in terms of storytelling and authorship. E.L. James's "Fifty Shades of Grey," originally self-published, exemplifies the impact of digital publishing on the genre, bringing erotic romance into mainstream consciousness and opening the door for more explicit content in romantic narratives.

This period has also been characterized by a significant blending of genres, with authors weaving elements of science fiction, fantasy, and thriller into their romance novels. This cross-pollination has given rise to sub-genres like paranormal romance and romantic suspense, broadening the appeal of contemporary romance to include readers of other genres. Authors like Kresley Cole with her "Immortals After Dark" series and Nalini Singh with her "Psy-Changeling" series have been instrumental in popularizing these blended genres, offering readers complex world-building alongside compelling romantic plots.

The Role of Diversity and Representation

In recent years, there has been a growing emphasis on diversity and representation within contemporary romance. Authors and readers alike are calling for stories that reflect a broader spectrum of experiences, including LGBTQ+ relationships, racial and cultural diversity, and characters with disabilities. This shift towards inclusivity has not only enriched the genre but also made it more reflective of the world today. Authors such as Alyssa Cole with her "Reluctant Royals" series and Helen Hoang with "The Kiss Quotient" have been at the forefront of this movement, showcasing the beauty and complexity of love in all its forms.

Chapter 1

Who's your Competition

The evolution of contemporary romance has been significantly shaped by pivotal bestselling authors whose works have not only defined but also expanded the genre. These authors have pushed the boundaries of contemporary romance, introducing new themes, diverse characters, and innovative narratives that reflect the complexities of modern love and society. If you want to write a contemporary romance that sells, I advise you to read these authors' books and study their style of writing.

Nora Roberts

Nora Roberts, often referred to as the "Queen of Romance," has been instrumental in defining contemporary romance's breadth and depth. With over 200 novels to her name,

Roberts has explored various facets of romance, from the idyllic small-town settings of her "Chesapeake Bay Saga" to the gripping suspense of her "In Death" series, written under the pseudonym J.D. Robb. Roberts' work is characterized by her ability to create compelling, emotionally resonant stories that capture the nuances of human relationships. Her success lies not just in her prolific output but in her skill at crafting narratives that resonate with readers seeking both escape and reflection on their own experiences.

Danielle Steel

Danielle Steel's contributions to contemporary romance are unparalleled in their exploration of themes like family, loss, and resilience against the backdrop of romantic relationships. Steel's novels often delve into the emotional landscapes of her characters, making her stories universally relatable. Her ability to tackle significant life events with sensitivity and depth has made her one of the bestselling authors in the genre. Steel's work reflects the changing dynamics of society and romance, offering narratives that span the globe and explore the spectrum of human emotion.

Helen Fielding

Helen Fielding's "Bridget Jones's Diary" marked a watershed moment for contemporary romance, introducing readers to a protagonist whose romantic misadventures and personal growth mirrored the lives of many modern women. Fielding's use of a diary format provided a candid, humorous insight into the everyday life of a single woman navigating the complexities of love in the 1990s. This novel, and its sequels, not only sparked a revival in romantic comedy but also highlighted the genre's potential to discuss issues of self-esteem, body image, and the societal pressure to find love.

Julia Quinn

Julia Quinn, best known for her historical romance series "The Bridgertons," has also made significant contributions to contemporary romance through her collaboration on projects like "The Lady Most Likely..." with fellow authors Eloisa James and Connie Brockway. Quinn's work, while primarily historical, has influenced contemporary romance by emphasizing strong, intelligent characters, witty dialogue, and emotionally charged narratives that appeal to modern sensibilities.

Colleen Hoover

A more recent figure in contemporary romance, Colleen Hoover, has brought a new level of emotional depth and complexity to the genre. Her novels, which often explore themes of love, loss, and redemption, have resonated with a younger generation of readers. Hoover's ability to tackle difficult subjects with honesty and sensitivity has seen her rise rapidly in popularity, marking a shift in contemporary romance towards more emotionally driven, issue-based narratives.

E.L. James

E.L. James' "Fifty Shades" series represents a significant milestone in contemporary romance, sparking a global conversation about erotic romance and its place in mainstream literature. Regardless of the varied critical reception, the series' success underscored readers' appetite for stories that push the boundaries of traditional romantic narratives, highlighting the genre's ability to evolve and cater to diverse preferences.

Sally Thorne

Sally Thorne burst onto the contemporary romance scene with "The Hating Game," a novel that quickly became a beloved romantic comedy for its witty banter, compelling character dynamics, and the engaging enemies-to-lovers trope. Thorne's ability to craft relatable, quirky characters and emotionally resonant narratives has made her a standout voice in the genre, capturing the complexities and humor of modern relationships.

Christina Lauren

Christina Lauren, the combined pen name of writing duo Christina Hobbs and Lauren Billings, has become synonymous with heartfelt and hilarious contemporary romance. With bestsellers like "Beautiful Bastard" and "The Unhoneymooners," they explore themes of love, friendship, and the unexpected paths to happiness. Their novels often feature strong, independent characters, snappy dialogue, and situations that resonate with contemporary issues and challenges, making their stories both entertaining and thought-provoking.

Helen Hoang

Helen Hoang has made a significant impact on contemporary romance with her nuanced portrayal of neurodiversity and her emphasis on diverse characters and experiences. Her debut novel, "The Kiss Quotient," introduces readers to a protagonist with Asperger's syndrome, offering a fresh perspective on romance and intimacy. Hoang's work is celebrated for its sensitivity, authenticity, and the way it broadens the representation of love in the genre.

.   .   .

Talia Hibbert

Talia Hibbert is a British author known for her inclusive, diverse, and body-positive romance novels that feature characters of various races, sizes, and social backgrounds. Her "Brown Sisters" series has been praised for its humor, emotional depth, and the representation of characters with chronic illnesses and disabilities. Hibbert's writing emphasizes the importance of love and relationships that celebrate acceptance and inclusivity.

Penelope Douglas

Penelope Douglas is renowned for her New Adult and contemporary romance novels that often explore darker themes within romantic relationships. Her books, including "Punk 57" and "Birthday Girl," delve into complex emotions and the more intense aspects of love, challenging traditional boundaries and expectations. Douglas's work appeals to readers looking for edgier, more provocative narratives.

Mariana Zapata

Mariana Zapata has earned a reputation as the queen of slow-burn romance, masterfully developing relationships that evolve gradually over the course of her novels. Her stories, such as "The Wall of Winnipeg and Me," focus on the buildup of emotional connections, making the eventual romantic culmination all the more satisfying. Zapata's work showcases the power of patience and depth in romantic storytelling.

Kennedy Ryan

Kennedy Ryan stands out for her emotionally charged novels and deep exploration of social issues within the framework of contemporary romance. Her books often tackle themes such as racial discrimination, disability, and empowerment, weaving these serious topics into the fabric of her love stories. Ryan's "Grip" series is particularly noted for its lyrical prose, complex characters, and the thoughtful handling of sensitive issues.

Vi Keeland and Penelope Ward

Vi Keeland and Penelope Ward, both successful in their own right, have also collaborated on several hit contemporary romance novels. Their works are known for engaging plots, dynamic characters, and the perfect blend of humor, heat, and heart. Books like "Stuck-Up Suit" and "Hate Notes" showcase their ability to co-create stories that are both entertaining and emotionally resonant.

· · ·

K.A. Tucker

K.A. Tucker is celebrated for her captivating storytelling and the ability to blend elements of mystery and suspense with deeply emotional romance narratives. Her "Ten Tiny Breaths" series and standalone novels like "The Simple Wild" highlight her skill at creating complex, multidimensional characters and settings that enhance the emotional stakes of her romantic plots.

Jasmine Guillory

Jasmine Guillory has quickly become a household name in contemporary romance with her delightful series of interconnected standalones, starting with "The Wedding Date." Guillory's writing is praised for its witty dialogue, charming characters, and the normalization of healthy romantic relationships. Her work stands out for its representation of African American protagonists and the seamless incorporation of contemporary social issues into engaging romantic stories.

Colleen Oakley

Colleen Oakley brings a unique twist to contemporary romance by infusing her stories with elements of magical realism and unconventional narrative choices. Her novels, such as "Before I Go" and "You Were There Too," offer poignant explorations of love, fate, and the choices that define us, making her a distinctive voice in the genre.

Emily Henry

Emily Henry has emerged as a star in contemporary romance with her bestselling novels "Beach Read" and "People We Meet on Vacation." Henry's writing is characterized by its depth, humor, and the exploration of themes like the complexity of relationships, personal growth, and the impact of past traumas on present love. Her ability to craft relatable, flawed characters who find love and understanding in each other has resonated with a wide audience.

Abby Jimenez

Abby Jimenez has made a notable impact with her heartfelt and humorous contemporary romances. Her debut, "The Friend Zone," tackles themes of love, friendship, and the complexities of infertility, blending emotional depth with relatable humor. Jimenez's ability to balance lighthearted moments with serious topics has endeared her to readers, making her books a staple for those who appreciate romance that mirrors the complexities of real life.

. . .

Alisha Rai

Alisha Rai is known for her modern and inclusive approach to contemporary romance. Her "Forbidden Hearts" series and "Modern Love" series explore themes of family, mental health, and consent, all while delivering compelling love stories. Rai's work is celebrated for its diversity, both in terms of character representation and the range of emotional experiences it portrays.

Alexis Hall

Alexis Hall has gained acclaim for his contributions to contemporary romance, particularly with "Boyfriend Material," a witty and touching M/M romance that explores themes of identity, family, and the search for authenticity in love. Hall's writing is characterized by its sharp humor, emotional intelligence, and the creation of deeply human characters whose journeys to love are both unique and universally relatable.

Lucy Score

Lucy Score's small-town romances and romantic comedies have captivated a large audience with their charm, humor, and engaging storylines. Her ability to create vibrant communities and relatable characters makes her books a comfort read for many. Titles like "Rock Bottom Girl" and "Pretend You're Mine" exemplify Score's talent for blending romantic escapism with realistic emotional conflicts.

Tessa Bailey

Tessa Bailey is renowned for her steamy, character-driven contemporary romances that often feature blue-collar heroes and strong, independent heroines. Her "Hot & Hammered" series, among others, showcases Bailey's knack for creating sizzling chemistry between her characters, combined with emotional depth and a touch of humor, making her books a favorite among readers looking for both heat and heart.

Beth O'Leary

Beth O'Leary quickly rose to prominence with "The Flatshare," a novel that combines a unique premise with endearing characters and a touching exploration of relationships and personal growth. O'Leary's approach to contemporary romance is notable for its originality, warmth, and the gentle way it tackles serious issues, providing readers with stories that are both uplifting and thought-provoking.

Casey McQuiston

Casey McQuiston's debut novel, "Red, White & Royal Blue," instantly captured the hearts of readers with its unique blend of humor, warmth, and political intrigue, wrapped around a compelling M/M romance. McQuiston's work is characterized by its optimistic portrayal of queer love, vibrant characters, and a storytelling style that blends emotional depth with pop culture savvy and sharp wit. Their subsequent novels continue to explore themes of identity, belonging, and the transformative power of love with a fresh and engaging approach.

Mhairi McFarlane

Mhairi McFarlane is a British author known for her witty, insightful, and emotionally rich contemporary romances. Her novels, such as "If I Never Met You" and "You Had Me at Hello," delve into the complexities of relationships, heartbreak, and finding love in unexpected places. McFarlane's work stands out for its relatable heroines, realistic portrayals of modern love, and the seamless integration of humor and heartache.

Sarah Morgan

Sarah Morgan has written numerous contemporary romances that range from holiday romances to deep emotional sagas set against the backdrop of various locales around the world. Her ability to craft engaging family dynamics, alongside swoon-worthy romances, makes her books a delightful escape. Morgan's storytelling is imbued with warmth, humor, and a deep understanding of human emotions, making her a favorite among fans of the genre.

Christina Lauren

Christina Lauren, the pen name for the writing duo Christina Hobbs and Lauren Billings, has been mentioned previously but deserves another nod for their substantial impact on contemporary romance. Their books, known for their dynamic characters, engaging plots, and perfect blend of humor and heat, cover a wide range of themes and settings, ensuring there's something for every romance reader in their extensive catalog.

Robyn Carr

Robyn Carr is best known for her Virgin River series, which has been adapted into a successful Netflix series. Carr's novels often explore the lives and loves of small-town communities, blending romance with elements of women's fiction. Her work is celebrated for its heartfelt storytelling, complex characters, and the sense of community and belonging that pervades her narratives

. . .

Jenny Han

Jenny Han, primarily known for her young adult fiction, notably the "To All the Boys I've Loved Before" series, has also made a significant impact on contemporary romance. Her YA novels, which explore first loves, family dynamics, and personal growth, resonate with readers of all ages. Han's ability to capture the sweetness and intensity of young love has endeared her to a broad audience, highlighting the crossover appeal of contemporary romance themes.

Chapter 2

Recurring Contemporary Romance Tropes

Contemporary romance, as a genre, thrives on its ability to mirror the complexities and idiosyncrasies of modern love through a variety of tropes and themes that resonate with readers. These elements serve as the backbone of the genre, offering a familiar yet versatile framework within which authors can explore the myriad facets of romance and relationships in the contemporary world. This chapter delves into the most prevalent tropes and themes, unpacking their significance and the ways in which they are continually reinvented to captivate the hearts and minds of readers.

1. Enemies to Lovers

One of the most beloved tropes, enemies to lovers thrives on the dynamic tension and eventual emotional payoff when two seemingly incompatible characters discover a deep connection. This trope explores themes of misunderstanding, personal growth, and the idea that love can flourish in the most unexpected soil. The journey from animosity to affection is often marked by witty banter, a gradual understanding of each other's true selves, and the dismantling of preconceived notions.

2. Friends to Lovers

In contrast to the fiery dynamic of enemies turning into lovers, the friends-to-lovers trope offers a warm exploration of love that blossoms from a foundation of friendship. This trope celebrates the depth of knowing someone thoroughly before romantic feelings emerge, highlighting the beauty of love that's rooted in mutual respect, shared history, and deep emotional connection. It speaks to the fantasy of falling in love with someone who already understands and cherishes you at your most authentic.

3. Fake Relationships

The fake relationship trope involves characters who, for various reasons, decide to enter into a pretend relationship. Whether it's to make an ex jealous, to secure a family inheritance, or to navigate a professional complication, this arrangement inevitably leads to genuine feelings. This trope plays with the idea of "pretend" as a safe space for characters to explore their feelings, often leading to realizations of love that surprise even them.

4. Second Chance Romance

Second chance romance taps into the longing and nostalgia for what once was, offering characters—and readers—a hopeful look at love's resilience over time and circumstance. This trope deals with lovers reuniting after a separation, giving them an opportunity to address past mistakes, misunderstandings, and growth. It's a testament to the enduring power of love and the belief that true love can overcome almost any obstacle.

5. Secret Romance

Secret romance focuses on relationships that, for one reason or another, must be kept hidden. This could be due to external pressures such as family disapproval, workplace rules, or social stigma. The secrecy adds an intensity to the relationship, with the hidden nature of the affair often heightening the emotional stakes and leading to a climactic reveal.

6. Grumpy One Loves the Sunshine One

This beloved trope contrasts two characters with diametrically opposed dispositions—the grumpy, often brooding character finds their match in a person of unwavering optimism and warmth. The dynamic between these characters is compelling, as the sunshine character often breaks through the grumpy one's barriers, revealing vulnerability and depth. This trope explores themes of emotional healing and the power of love to bring light into darkness, resonating deeply with readers who appreciate the transformative impact of relationships.

7. Opposites Attract

Closely related to the grumpy and sunshine dynamic, the opposites attract trope plays on the magnetic pull between characters who, on the surface, seem entirely mismatched. Whether it's differing personalities, lifestyles, or backgrounds, these differences create a rich ground for conflict, growth, and ultimately, a deep and unexpected connection. This trope celebrates the idea that love can bridge divides, offering a hopeful message about finding common ground and mutual respect.

8. Forced Proximity

Forced proximity throws characters into situations where they must spend a significant amount of time together, often in close quarters. This could be due to a snowstorm, a work assignment, or any scenario that requires them to share space. The close interaction accelerates the relationship development, highlighting the characters' chemistry and deepening their bond. This trope is particularly effective in contemporary romance for exploring the nuances of falling in love when there's no escape from being together.

9. Return to Hometown

Many contemporary romances feature protagonists returning to their hometowns, where they're confronted with past relationships, unresolved conflicts, and often, a second chance at love. This trope taps into the nostalgia and introspection that accompany a return to one's roots, offering a backdrop for characters to reassess what truly matters. The hometown setting often brings a sense of community and belonging, adding depth to the romantic narrative.

10. Fake Engagement or Marriage

A variant of the fake relationship trope, fake engagements or marriages up the ante by entangling characters in scenarios that require a deeper commitment to maintain the facade. Whether it's to appease family, secure an inheritance, or achieve a professional goal, these arrangements invariably lead to genuine feelings and complicated entanglements. This trope explores themes of honesty, vulnerability, and the unexpected paths to love.

11. Workplace Romance

Workplace romances explore the complexities of navigating romantic feelings in a professional setting. From office rivalries turning into love to relationships between bosses and their employees, this trope delves into the power dynamics, ethical considerations, and emotional stakes involved in mixing business with pleasure. Workplace romances reflect contemporary issues around career, ambition, and the search for balance between personal and professional life.

12. Redemption and Forgiveness

This trope centers on characters who have made mistakes or wronged others in the past and are on a path to redemption. Their journey often involves earning forgiveness from those they've hurt, including love interests. These stories delve into themes of growth, accountability, and the healing power of love, resonating with readers who believe in second chances and the capacity for change.

13. Single Parent and Nanny

Romances involving single parents and nannies (or other caregivers) explore the dynamics of family, responsibility, and the blending of professional and personal boundaries. These narratives often highlight themes of trust, the challenges of parenting, and the formation of unconventional families, offering a heartwarming look at the ways love can expand to include not just the couple but the children as well.

14. Love Triangle

The love triangle trope involves a character faced with choosing between two potential love interests, each representing different paths or aspects of desire. This trope delves into themes of conflict, desire, and decision-making, highlighting the protagonist's emotional journey towards understanding their true feelings. Love triangles can add tension and drama to the narrative, making the eventual choice all the more satisfying for the reader.

15. Amnesia

Amnesia in contemporary romance explores the fallout and rediscovery of love when one character loses their memories of the relationship. This trope allows for a fresh exploration of love between established partners, posing questions about the nature of love and identity. It's a compelling way to explore themes of trust, loyalty, and the foundational aspects of love that persist beyond memory.

16. Road Trip

The road trip trope takes characters on a journey, both literal and metaphorical, as they travel together. This setting is ripe for forced proximity, character development, and the exploration of themes like freedom, discovery, and the transformative power of shared experiences. The changing backdrops and adventures along the way serve as catalysts for the characters to open up, confront their issues, and fall in love.

17. Marriage of Convenience

Similar to fake engagements or marriages, the marriage of convenience trope revolves around characters who marry for practical reasons rather than love. These reasons can range from financial benefits to immigration issues, creating a scenario where the characters are forced to navigate married life together. This trope explores how love can grow from partnership and mutual respect, often leading to genuine feelings and emotional intimacy.

18. Healing/Recovery

Romances centered around healing or recovery often feature characters dealing with physical, emotional, or psychological wounds. The love interest may play a key role in their recovery, offering support, understanding, and unconditional love. This trope delves into themes of vulnerability, strength, and the healing power of love, showcasing how relationships can contribute to personal growth and healing.

19. Small Town Romance

Set against the backdrop of close-knit communities, small town romances explore the dynamics of returning to or discovering new life in a small town. These stories often highlight themes of belonging, community support, and the charm of simpler living, juxtaposed with the challenges of gossip, tradition, and the past. The small town setting provides a unique canvas for romance, where relationships are deeply intertwined with community life.

20. Sports Romance

Sports romances focus on characters involved in the world of sports, whether they're athletes, coaches, or related to the sports industry in some capacity. These stories often explore themes of ambition, competition, and the balance between professional commitments and personal life. The backdrop of sports provides a dynamic setting for romance, characterized by physicality, teamwork, and the pursuit of excellence.

21. Holiday Romance

Holiday romances capitalize on the magic and romance of the holiday season, setting up scenarios where love blossoms against the backdrop of Christmas, New Year's Eve, Valentine's Day, or other significant holidays. These stories often explore themes of renewal, joy, and the spirit of giving, offering readers a festive escape into worlds where love is especially poignant and transformative.

22. Accidental Pregnancy

Accidental pregnancy in contemporary romance introduces unexpected dynamics into the relationship, compelling characters to navigate the complexities of unplanned parenthood together. This trope explores themes of responsibility, commitment, and the ways in which a surprise pregnancy can accelerate intimacy and emotional growth between the characters. It's a potent scenario for character development, as they confront their fears, hopes, and the future they want to build.

23. Best Friend's Sibling

The allure of forbidden romance is at the heart of the best friend's sibling trope, where a character falls for their friend's brother or sister. This scenario is ripe with potential conflict, loyalty tests, and the fear of jeopardizing important relationships for love. It delves into themes of forbidden desire, the boundaries of friendship, and the risks we take for love, often leading to secretive liaisons and the eventual need for acceptance and understanding.

24. Disguise and Secret Identities

Characters hiding their true identities, whether for protection, investigation, or to escape their past, add layers of intrigue and mystery to the romance. As these characters interact under the guise of their assumed identities, the trope explores themes of authenticity, trust, and the discovery of love in unexpected places. The revelation of true identities provides dramatic moments that test the relationship's foundation and the characters' acceptance of each other's realities.

25. Age Gap Romance

Age gap romance addresses the dynamics and challenges of a significant age difference between the couple. This trope explores societal perceptions, power imbalances, and the unique conflicts that arise from differing life stages. It's a fertile ground for examining themes of maturity, life experience, and the timeless nature of love, challenging the characters (and readers) to look beyond numbers and focus on the connection that binds the couple.

26. Royalty/Commoner

The romance between a royal and a commoner brings the fantasy of fairy tales into contemporary settings, exploring the clash of worlds, duties, and public scrutiny. This trope delves into themes of duty versus desire, the sacrifices required for love, and the challenges of bridging vastly different lifestyles. It's a narrative that captivates with its blend of glamour, secrecy, and the universal quest for happiness beyond societal roles.

27. Protector/Guardian

In these stories, one character is tasked with protecting the other, setting the stage for a deep emotional connection forged in the face of danger. This trope examines themes of safety, trust, and the protective instincts that can spark and fuel attraction. It highlights the strength and vulnerability of both the protector and the one being protected, creating a dynamic interplay of power, responsibility, and love.

28. Reunited Lovers

Reunited lovers focus on characters who had a past relationship and, after years apart, come back into each other's lives. This trope allows for exploration of themes related to forgiveness, the impact of time on love, and the possibility of reigniting old flames under new circumstances. It offers a poignant look at how people change and grow, and how true love can endure time's test.

29. Soulmates/Fated Lovers

The concept of soulmates or fated lovers speaks to the idea of a deep, predestined connection between two people. This trope explores the magnetic pull between the characters, the sense of inevitability in their coming together, and the challenges they face to be with one another. It delves into themes of destiny, the power of connection, and the belief in a love that transcends ordinary understanding.

30. Celebrity/Commoner

Romances involving a celebrity and a non-famous person navigate the complexities of public life versus private happiness. This trope examines the pressures of fame, the quest for authenticity, and the sacrifices required to maintain a relationship in the public eye. It's a narrative that juxtaposes the glittering allure of celebrity with the universal desires for love, understanding, and a genuine connection.

As you embark on your journey through the vibrant landscape of contemporary romance, remember that these tropes are more than just familiar plots or scenarios. They are canvases upon which you can paint the rich, intricate stories of love that beat with the pulse of our times. Each trope, from the whirlwind of accidental pregnancies to the fairytale allure of royalty and commoner romances, offers you a unique opportunity to delve into the human heart. They allow you to explore the depths of desire, the complexities of relationships, and the infinite facets of emotion that love can evoke.

Consider these tropes as your toolkit, your palette of colors with which to draw readers into worlds where love transcends the mundane and transforms the ordinary into something utterly extraordinary. As you wield these tools, infuse your narratives with authenticity and emotional truth. Let your characters breathe, live, and love with a realism that leaps off the page and captures the hearts of your readers.

Remember, it's not just about the tropes themselves but how you, with your unique voice and perspective, choose to reinterpret them. The magic lies in your ability to take these well-worn paths and sprinkle them with your own brand of creativity, insight, and human experience. This is where the true artistry of contemporary romance writing lies.

In your hands, a simple story of reunited lovers can become a poignant exploration of growth and forgiveness. A celebrity/commoner romance can transform into a profound commentary on identity, privacy, and the true cost of fame. With each word you write, you have the power to challenge, to entertain, and to illuminate the myriad ways in which we seek connection, understanding, and, ultimately, love.

So, as you craft your stories, let these tropes guide you but not confine you. Play with them, twist them, turn them on their heads if you must. Your goal is to create tales that resonate, that echo with the truths of our shared human experience, and that remind us all of the transformative power of love. In doing so, you'll not only captivate your readers but also contribute to the ever-evolving tapestry of contemporary romance. Remember, the heart of your story lies not in the trope you choose but in the humanity you infuse it with. Write with courage, write with passion, and, above all, write with love.

Chapter 3

Common Themes in Contemporary Romances

As you dive into the rich and multifaceted world of contemporary romance, it's essential to recognize the powerful undercurrents that give depth and resonance to the stories we tell and cherish. Beyond the allure of tropes and the intricate dance of plotlines lies the soul of any narrative: its themes. Themes in contemporary romance are the universal truths, the shared experiences, and the emotional journeys that connect the reader's heart to the characters' lives. They are the backbone of storytelling, providing insight, evoking empathy, and often reflecting the complexities of our own realities.

In this exploration of themes in contemporary romance, we delve into the recurring motifs that define and enrich the genre. From the transformative power of love and personal growth to the challenges of navigating societal pressures and the quest for identity, these themes offer a canvas for authors to explore the nuances of human emotion, relationship dynamics, and the quest for a happy ending in the modern world. Whether you're a budding writer or a seasoned author, understanding these themes is crucial to crafting stories that resonate deeply with your audience, inviting them to see their hopes, fears, and dreams reflected in the pages of your work.

As we embark on this journey together, remember that the true artistry of contemporary romance writing lies not just in the stories you choose to tell, but in how you illuminate the themes within them. Your voice has the power to illuminate, to challenge, and to heal. Let's explore the themes that serve as the heartbeat of contemporary romance, guiding your creative process and connecting your stories to the very essence of the human experience.

1. Personal Growth and Healing

Contemporary romance frequently explores the theme of personal growth, with characters often embarking on journeys of self-discovery and healing alongside their romantic endeavors. These narratives emphasize the idea that love can be a transformative force, encouraging individuals to confront their past, overcome their fears, and embrace their true selves.

2. Family Dynamics and Community

The backdrop of family and community plays a significant role in contemporary romance, highlighting the impact of these relationships on the protagonists' romantic lives. Stories may delve into the complexities of familial expectations, the support system provided by close-knit communities, or the challenges of navigating love in the face of family drama.

3. Social Issues and Cultural Identity

Increasingly, contemporary romance is addressing social issues and cultural identity, weaving these themes into the fabric of the love story. Authors are tackling topics such as racial inequality, LGBTQ+ rights, mental health, and more, providing a more inclusive and realistic portrayal of romance that reflects the diverse world we live in.

4. Career and Ambition

The balancing act between career ambitions and romantic aspirations is a common theme, reflecting modern society's emphasis on professional success and personal fulfillment. These stories explore the challenges and compromises involved in striving for both love and career achievements, often leading to a reevaluation of what truly matters.

5. Technological Influence on Romance

With the digital age reshaping how we connect and communicate, contemporary romance is increasingly incorporating the impact of technology on relationships. From online dating to long-distance love maintained through video calls, this theme examines the opportunities and challenges presented by modern communication methods in the pursuit of love.

6. Identity and Self-Discovery

In the tapestry of contemporary romance, the theme of identity and self-discovery often takes center stage, providing a rich ground for character development and emotional depth. This theme explores the journey of characters as they navigate the complexities of who they are and who they wish to become, often influenced by their relationships and the challenges they face. It's a reminder that love, in its most transformative capacity, can act as a mirror, reflecting our truest selves and pushing us towards self-acceptance and growth.

7. Societal Expectations and Norms

The clash between individual desires and societal expectations is a recurring theme that resonates deeply within contemporary romance. Characters often grapple with the pressures of conforming to societal norms, whether it's in regards to their career choices, romantic relationships, or lifestyle decisions. This theme invites readers to question and reflect on the external forces shaping their lives, championing the courage it takes to defy expectations in pursuit of personal happiness.

8. Communication and Miscommunication

At the heart of many contemporary romances lies the theme of communication, or often, the lack thereof. Miscommunication serves as a pivotal plot device, driving the conflict and tension between characters. Conversely, effective communication is celebrated as the key to resolving conflict and deepening connections. This theme underscores the importance of honesty, vulnerability, and the sometimes difficult journey towards understanding and being understood within relationships.

9. Forgiveness and Redemption

Forgiveness and redemption are powerful themes that explore the capacity for characters to move beyond past mistakes and hurt, both in themselves and in others. These narratives often delve into the complexities of forgiveness, questioning what it means to forgive and highlighting the healing power of love and understanding. Redemption arcs offer characters a path to make amends, showcasing the transformative impact of love and the possibility of second chances.

10. Balance Between Career and Personal Life

The struggle to balance career ambitions with personal relationships is a theme that mirrors the contemporary dilemma many face. Characters are often depicted juggling the demands of their professional lives with the needs of their personal relationships, leading to tension, conflict, and ultimately, growth. This theme resonates with readers who themselves are navigating the delicate balance between achieving professional success and nurturing personal connections.

11. Diversity and Inclusivity

Contemporary romance increasingly embraces diversity and inclusivity, reflecting the rich tapestry of human experience across cultures, ethnicities, sexual orientations, and more. This theme celebrates the beauty of love in all its forms, challenging traditional romance narratives to include a broader range of voices and stories. It's a call to recognize and honor the diverse ways in which people find love and connection, enriching the genre with more authentic and varied perspectives.

Chapter 4

Tropes that Sell

In the world of contemporary romance, certain tropes have proven their allure time and again, captivating readers and topping bestseller lists. These tropes, with their familiar yet endlessly versatile narratives, provide a foundation upon which some of the most memorable and beloved romance stories are built. Let's dive into specific tropes that have a strong track record of success, highlighting examples from bestselling and critically acclaimed works that have captured the hearts of readers worldwide.

1. Enemies to Lovers

The enemies to lovers trope is a perennial favorite, drawing readers in with the promise of intense emotional journeys and the irresistible transformation of animosity into love. This trope thrives on the tension and chemistry between the protagonists, making their eventual romantic connection all the more satisfying.

Example: "The Hating Game" by Sally Thorne is a quintessential enemies-to-lovers story that pits Lucy Hutton against her office nemesis, Joshua Templeman. Their banter and battles of wits provide a delicious buildup to a love story that's both heartwarming and humor-filled, showcasing the trope's enduring appeal.

2. Fake Relationships

Fake relationships, ranging from fake dating to fake engagements, offer a delightful premise where characters pretend to be in love for various reasons, only to find themselves falling for real. This trope explores themes of authenticity, vulnerability, and the unexpected paths to love.

Example: "To All the Boys I've Loved Before" by Jenny Han brilliantly employs this trope through Lara Jean Covey and Peter Kavinsky's fake relationship. Designed to make Peter's ex-girlfriend jealous and to allay Lara Jean's romantic dilemmas, their pretense gradually unveils genuine feelings, illustrating the trope's power to blend playfulness with emotional depth.

3. Second Chance Romance

Second chance romance speaks to the hope of rediscovered love, focusing on couples who reunite after time apart. It resonates with readers through themes of forgiveness, growth, and the idea that true love can endure and evolve.

Example: "It Ends with Us" by Colleen Hoover, while not a traditional second chance romance, incorporates elements of this trope through its complex exploration of past and present relationships. The novel delves into the protagonists' reevaluation of love and the possibility of new beginnings, highlighting the trope's relevance to real-life complexities.

4. Friends to Lovers

The friends to lovers trope celebrates the deep, underlying connection that exists between long-standing friends who discover romantic feelings for one another. It's a testament to the beauty of love that blossoms from friendship, marked by trust, mutual respect, and a profound understanding of each other.

Example: "Josh and Hazel's Guide to Not Dating" by Christina Lauren is a heartwarming depiction of this trope. Josh and Hazel's transition from friends to lovers is filled with humor, misadventures, and the realization that they are perfect for each other, embodying the trope's charm and the seamless blend of friendship and romance.

5. Forbidden Love

Forbidden love stories, with their inherent tension and stakes, captivate readers with tales of love that defies societal rules, family expectations, or external constraints. This trope explores the lengths to which people will go for love, often leading to powerful, emotional narratives.

Example: "The Seven Husbands of Evelyn Hugo" by Taylor Jenkins Reid, though not a traditional contemporary romance, incorporates elements of forbidden love through its exploration of Hollywood icon Evelyn Hugo's secret love affairs. The novel addresses themes of identity, sacrifice, and the pursuit of love against all odds, showcasing the trope's ability to tackle deep, emotional truths.

6. Grumpy One Loves the Sunshine One

The dynamic between a grumpy, often closed-off character and their polar opposite, a sunshine-filled, eternally optimistic one, offers a rich ground for exploration in contemporary romance. This trope delights in the contrast and eventual convergence of differing worldviews, showcasing how opposites not only attract but can profoundly transform one another.

Example: "The Unhoneymooners" by Christina Lauren epitomizes this trope through the characters of Olive and Ethan. Olive's relentless positivity clashes with Ethan's more cynical outlook, leading to a romance that's as comedic as it is heartfelt. Their journey from antagonists to lovers highlights the trope's appeal in showcasing growth and understanding through love.

7. Return to Hometown

Characters returning to their hometowns often face unresolved pasts, old flames, or family conflicts, setting the stage for romance that's interwoven with themes of redemption, reconciliation, and self-discovery. This trope resonates with readers through its exploration of coming home in both a literal and metaphorical sense.

Example: "The Best Thing" by Mariana Zapata presents this trope through the story of Lenny, who returns to her hometown and confronts unresolved feelings for Jonah, a man from her past. The slow burn romance that ensues is a testament to the trope's ability to blend personal growth with the rekindling of old flames.

8. Workplace Romance

The workplace romance trope explores the complexities of romantic involvement in a professional setting, addressing the balance of power, ethics, and the blending of personal and professional lives. It's a fertile ground for tension, drama, and the exploration of boundaries.

Example: "Beautiful Bastard" by Christina Lauren is a standout example of this trope, featuring a contentious and steamy relationship between Chloe, an ambitious intern, and Bennett, her exacting boss. Their story navigates the complications and ethical dilemmas of a workplace romance, providing a compelling narrative of passion, conflict, and love.

9. Single Parent Romance

Romances involving single parents add layers of depth to the narrative, introducing themes of responsibility, blended families, and the challenges of dating with children. This trope appeals to readers through its realistic portrayal of love in the context of parenthood and family dynamics.

Example: "Look the Part" by Jewel E. Ann centers on Flint, a single father, and Ellen, his tenant, who forms a connection with both Flint and his son. The story beautifully navigates the complexities of falling in love while prioritizing the well-being of children, illustrating the trope's capacity for emotional richness and layered storytelling.

10. Forced Proximity

Forced proximity scenarios, where characters are compelled to share close quarters, accelerate the romance by creating an environment ripe for intimacy to flourish. Whether stranded together, cohabiting for convenience, or partnering on a project, this trope capitalizes on the tension and inevitable closeness that arises.

Example: "The Deal" by Elle Kennedy showcases this trope through Hannah and Garrett, who strike a bargain that leads to unexpected cohabitation and collaboration. The forced proximity serves as a catalyst for their relationship, highlighting the trope's effectiveness in building romantic tension and deepening connections.

11. Sports Romance

Sports romances delve into the lives of athletes and those connected to the world of sports, offering a backdrop of competition, physicality, and the pursuit of excellence. This trope explores themes of ambition, teamwork, and the intersection of personal and professional lives in the context of romantic relationships.

Example: "The Wall of Winnipeg and Me" by Mariana Zapata tells the story of Vanessa and Aiden, an assistant and her professional football player boss. Their slow-building romance, set against the backdrop of the demanding world of professional sports, exemplifies the trope's ability to combine passion for the game with the development of a deep, enduring love.

Chapter 5

Strategies for combining tropes in unconventional ways to craft unique and compelling narratives

Mixing and matching tropes in contemporary romance is akin to a culinary art—combining familiar ingredients in unexpected ways to create a dish that surprises and delights the palate. This approach allows authors to craft unique and compelling narratives that stand out in a crowded market. Here are strategies for blending tropes to breathe new life into your stories:

1. Identify Compatible Tropes

Start by listing tropes that interest you, then explore their compatibility. Some tropes naturally complement each other, like fake relationships and enemies to lovers, creating a dynamic story arc filled with tension and eventual resolution. However, the real magic happens when you pair seemingly incompatible tropes, like a second chance romance with a supernatural twist, offering readers both the comfort of familiarity and the thrill of the unexpected.

2. Focus on Character Development

Character development is key when mixing tropes. Each trope brings its own set of expectations regarding character behavior and growth. By focusing on how the characters are shaped by their unique circumstances, you can seamlessly integrate different tropes. For instance, combining the grumpy one loves the sunshine one trope with a forced proximity scenario provides ample opportunity for character exploration and growth, revealing depths and vulnerabilities that enrich the narrative.

3. Create a Cohesive Plot

Ensure that the combination of tropes serves the plot in a cohesive and logical manner. The plot should not feel like a mere backdrop for the tropes but rather the driving force that weaves them together. For example, a return to hometown trope mixed with a secret baby storyline can offer a compelling narrative if the plot carefully navigates the emotional and logistical complexities of these situations, leading to a satisfying resolution that feels earned.

4. Innovate Within the Trope Framework

Look for ways to innovate within each trope. Consider flipping traditional gender roles, setting the story in an unconventional location, or adding a genre twist, like a mystery to solve in a friends to lovers scenario. This not only refreshes the tropes but also creates a narrative that defies expectations and engages readers in a new way.

5. Balance the Tropes

When mixing tropes, balance is crucial. Avoid allowing one trope to overshadow the other; each should contribute to the story's emotional and narrative depth. This balance ensures that the story remains engaging and that readers can appreciate the unique way the tropes interact and complement each other.

6. Use Subversion to Surprise Readers

Subverting one or both tropes can add an element of surprise that captivates readers. If you're blending the fake relationship trope with the workplace romance trope, consider how you can subvert expectations within those frameworks. Perhaps the fake relationship is not to make an ex jealous but to challenge corporate policies against workplace relationships, adding layers of commentary and conflict.

7. Integrate Themes for Depth

Incorporate themes that resonate across the chosen tropes to add depth to your story. Themes such as redemption, identity, or the search for belonging can tie disparate tropes together, giving your narrative a thematic richness that enhances the emotional stakes and connects with readers on a deeper level.

8. Test and Iterate

Don't be afraid to experiment with different combinations in your writing process. Some mixes might not work as well as others, but through testing and iteration, you'll find the perfect blend that tells the story you want to share. Feedback from beta readers can be invaluable in this process, providing insight into how effectively the tropes are combined and the overall coherence of the narrative.

9. Leverage Setting and World-Building

The setting of your story can act as a catalyst for merging tropes in innovative ways. Utilize your story's environment to bring together tropes that might not traditionally interact. For instance, a sports romance (trope) set in a dystopian future (world-building) could intersect with a survival of the fittest theme, where love blossoms in the midst of competition for survival. This approach not only provides a fresh backdrop for the romance but also allows for unique challenges and growth opportunities for your characters.

10. Introduce External Conflicts

Introducing an external conflict can serve as an effective method for blending tropes. For example, combining the small-town romance trope with a suspense element, such as a mystery the protagonists need to solve together, adds an additional layer of tension and stakes to the relationship. This not only heightens the drama but also allows for natural intersections of character development, as each trope influences how they navigate challenges together.

11. Play with Narrative Structure

Experimenting with the narrative structure can offer creative ways to mix tropes. Consider non-linear storytelling, multiple points of view, or epistolary elements (like letters or diary entries) to weave together tropes such as second chance romance and secret romance. This method can reveal the depth of the characters' past relationships and secrets, building anticipation and complexity as the story unfolds.

12. Incorporate Cultural Elements

Drawing on diverse cultural elements can enrich the trope mix, offering new dimensions to explore. A contemporary romance that combines the arranged marriage trope with a cross-cultural exchange can delve into themes of identity, tradition, and adaptation. This approach not only diversifies the narrative but also provides a platform for exploring how cultural backgrounds influence and enrich the romantic journey.

13. Utilize Side Characters

Side characters can play a pivotal role in bringing together disparate tropes. Through their interactions, backstories, or subplots, you can seamlessly integrate and juxtapose main tropes. For instance, the main story might follow an enemies to lovers arc, while side characters could be navigating a friends to lovers scenario. This juxtaposition can offer contrast, highlight different aspects of relationships, and enrich the main narrative with parallel themes.

14. Embrace Emotional Complexity

Mixing tropes successfully often involves embracing and depicting emotional complexity. By allowing characters to navigate the internal conflicts that arise from blended tropes —such as the fear of opening up in a fake relationship that becomes real—authors can create deeply resonant and multifaceted narratives. This emotional depth ensures that the combination of tropes feels not only innovative but also authentic and compelling.

15. Challenge Genre Boundaries

Don't be afraid to challenge the boundaries of the romance genre itself. Mixing tropes from different genres—such as a romantic comedy with a sci-fi adventure—can result in a story that's as surprising as it is engaging. This strategy encourages authors to think outside the traditional confines of contemporary romance and explore how love and rela-tionships might look in different narrative landscapes.

16. Focus on the Journey

Finally, the key to successfully mixing tropes lies in focusing on the characters' journey. Regardless of how many tropes you weave together, the heart of the story should always be the characters' emotional and relational development. This focus ensures that, no matter how unconventional the trope combination, the narrative remains grounded in the universal themes of love, growth, and connection that define the best of contemporary romance.

By applying these strategies, authors can craft narratives that are not only unique but also deeply engaging, offering readers a fresh take on the beloved tropes of contemporary romance. This creative mixing and matching not only enrich the genre but also demonstrate the limitless possibilities for storytelling within the vast landscape of romantic fiction.

Chapter 6

Creating Relatable Characters

In the heart of every memorable contemporary romance lies a cast of characters that readers can see themselves in, empathize with, or aspire to be like. Creating relatable characters is a cornerstone of crafting stories that resonate, linger in the mind long after the last page is turned, and ultimately, connect on a deep emotional level with the audience. This chapter delves into the art and craft of bringing to life characters that embody the complexities, desires, and struggles of real people navigating the waters of modern love.

Understanding Relatability

To start, understanding what makes a character relatable is key. Relatability doesn't mean your characters must mirror every reader's experience or personality. Instead, it's about capturing the essence of human emotion and experience in a way that transcends the specifics of your characters' lives. It's in their desires, fears, failures, and triumphs that readers find pieces of themselves or insights into others.

Diversity and Representation

One of the most significant shifts in contemporary romance has been the move towards more inclusive and diverse representations. Characters from a range of backgrounds, cultures, orientations, and life experiences not only reflect the world more accurately but also enrich the narrative tapestry of romance literature. Crafting characters with diverse identities requires research, empathy, and a commitment to portraying experiences authentically and respectfully.

Flawed Yet Lovable Characters

Perfection is not only unattainable but also unrelatable. Characters with flaws, insecurities, and mistakes are infinitely more engaging than their flawless counterparts. These imperfections make characters feel real and give them room to grow, which is a journey readers love to witness. The key is to balance their flaws with redeeming qualities or vulnerabilities that evoke empathy and understanding.

Character Backstories

A well-developed backstory adds depth to your characters, influencing their motivations, fears, and desires in the narrative present. Understanding where your characters come from—both literally and figuratively—allows you to craft responses and growth arcs that feel true to their experiences. A rich backstory also provides fertile ground for conflict and resolution within the romance, driving emotional engagement.

Dynamic Character Relationships

The interactions between your characters can significantly enhance their relatability. Dynamic relationships that evolve over time, whether fraught with tension, filled with humor, or marked by mutual support, reflect the complexities of real-life relationships. These interactions also offer opportunities to showcase different facets of your characters, making them more rounded and engaging.

Emotional Resonance

At the core of relatability is emotional resonance—the ability of your characters' experiences, thoughts, and feelings to strike a chord with readers. Crafting moments of vulnerability, joy, heartbreak, and love that feel genuine requires a deep understanding of human emotion and the skill to express it compellingly. These emotionally resonant moments are what readers remember and connect with most deeply.

Growth and Change

A character's growth journey is often what makes them most relatable. Witnessing characters confront challenges, evolve, and emerge transformed is a powerful narrative force. This journey doesn't need to be dramatic to be impactful; even subtle shifts in understanding, acceptance, or perspective can offer profound insights into the human condition.

Voice and Point of View

The narrative voice and chosen point of view (POV) play crucial roles in how characters are perceived and related to by readers. A strong, distinctive voice can make characters leap off the page, while the POV—whether first person, close third, or alternating perspectives—can deeply influence how intimately readers connect with the characters' inner worlds.

Chapter 7

Crafting Protagonists: The Heart of Contemporary Romance

In the realm of contemporary romance, the protagonists are the soul of the story, guiding readers through a journey of love, conflict, and transformation. Crafting protagonists involves more than just sketching out a character with appealing traits; it's about creating multidimensional beings who reflect the diversity and complexity of real life. These characters must resonate with readers, evoking empathy, inspiration, and a profound sense of connection. The importance of such character creation cannot be overstated, for it is through these protagonists that a narrative finds its heart and its voice.

A protagonist in contemporary romance should be as layered and multifaceted as the people we encounter in our lives. They should possess a blend of strengths and vulnerabilities, dreams and doubts, making them relatable and real.

This depth of character allows readers to see parts of themselves in the story, fostering a deeper engagement with the narrative. Moreover, it's through the protagonists' flaws and growth that the story often finds its most compelling arcs. The journey of overcoming personal obstacles, learning to embrace one's imperfections, and growing from experiences is a narrative that mirrors the human condition, making the story not just a tale of romance but a reflection on life itself.

Equally important is the representation of diversity through these characters. Contemporary romance thrives on its ability to tell a wide range of stories, reflecting the rich tapestry of humanity. By crafting protagonists from various backgrounds, cultures, orientations, and walks of life, authors can offer a more inclusive and authentic exploration of love and relationships. This diversity not only enriches the genre but also ensures that more readers can see themselves and their experiences reflected in these love stories. It challenges the genre to evolve, pushing it towards more nuanced and representative narratives that speak to a global audience.

Moreover, the complexity of real people extends beyond their individual traits to how they interact with the world and the people around them. A well-crafted protagonist in contemporary romance navigates a web of relationships—be it family, friends, or romantic interests—that shape their journey and define their growth. These interactions offer opportunities to explore the dynamics of human relationships, the challenges of communication and misunderstanding, and the beauty of connection and reconciliation. Through these relational dynamics, protagonists become mirrors reflecting the multifarious nature of love and companionship in the modern world.

In essence, the crafting of protagonists in contemporary romance is an exercise in empathy, creativity, and authenticity. It demands a deep understanding of human nature and a commitment to portraying it in all its diversity and complexity. These characters, with their dreams, struggles, and journeys, become the vehicles through which readers explore the landscapes of love, change, and self-discovery. By emphasizing the creation of multidimensional characters who capture the breadth of human experience, contemporary romance continues to offer stories that not only entertain but also resonate deeply with readers, reminding them of the transformative power of love in all its forms.

Chapter 8

Address the Necessity of Inclusivity and Diversity

The contemporary romance genre serves as a mirror to society, reflecting the complexities, challenges, and joys of modern love. As such, diversity and representation within these narratives are not just beneficial but essential. They ensure that the genre is inclusive, offering a window into the myriad ways love manifests across different cultures, identities, and experiences. The necessity of inclusivity in contemporary romance is paramount for crafting stories that resonate with a broad audience, fostering empathy, understanding, and respect among readers. This commitment to diversity enriches the genre, making it more vibrant and reflective of the world we inhabit.

To achieve authentic and respectful representation, authors must first acknowledge the wide range of human experiences and the importance of portraying them with integrity.

This involves moving beyond stereotypes and superficial characterizations to delve into the nuanced realities of individuals from diverse backgrounds. It's about telling stories that respect the complexity of people's lives, their cultures, and their identities. For instance, Helen Hoang's "The Kiss Quotient" is celebrated for its sensitive and nuanced portrayal of a neurodiverse protagonist, offering readers insight into the experiences of someone on the autism spectrum while delivering a compelling love story.

Research plays a crucial role in crafting narratives that authentically represent diverse experiences. This means going beyond cursory internet searches to engage with primary sources, including books, documentaries, and first-hand accounts from people who directly experience the realities being portrayed. For authors writing outside their own experiences, consulting with sensitivity readers can provide invaluable insights and help avoid unintentional harm or misrepresentation. Alyssa Cole's "A Princess in Theory" exemplifies thorough research and cultural sensitivity, blending romance with elements that respect and celebrate African cultures, setting a high bar for authentic representation.

Inclusivity in contemporary romance also means challenging and expanding the genre's traditional boundaries. This involves exploring stories that center on characters from marginalized communities, including those of different races, ethnicities, sexual orientations, gender identities, physical abilities, and more. Casey McQuiston's "Red, White & Royal Blue" demonstrates how a romance between two men from politically significant families can not only captivate readers but also challenge societal norms and expectations about love and identity.

Another key aspect of inclusivity is ensuring that diverse characters are depicted with agency, depth, and as protagonists of their own stories. They should not exist merely to support the narratives of more traditionally represented characters but should be fully realized individuals whose journeys are central to the plot. This approach allows for a richer, more engaging reading experience that honors the depth of human diversity. Talia Hibbert's work, such as "Get a Life, Chloe Brown," is a testament to creating characters with agency and depth, showcasing how romance can thrive in narratives centered around Black women and individuals with chronic illnesses.

Dialogue and collaboration with communities represented in romance narratives are essential for authentic inclusivity. Engaging with these communities can provide deeper insights, highlight potential blind spots, and foster a more respectful and accurate portrayal of diverse experiences. This collaborative approach not only enhances the authenticity of the representation but also builds bridges between authors and the communities they depict, creating a more inclusive literary landscape.

Moreover, inclusivity and representation should be woven into the fabric of the narrative naturally and purposefully, avoiding tokenism or the reduction of characters to mere aspects of their identity. Inclusivity should enrich the story, contributing to its depth and complexity, rather than serving as a checkbox of diversity. Mariana Zapata's "The Wall of Winnipeg and Me" integrates cultural diversity seamlessly into its narrative, enriching the story without reducing characters to stereotypes or their cultural background.

The goal of inclusivity in contemporary romance is to tell stories that acknowledge, respect, and celebrate the diversity of human experience. By doing so authentically and respectfully, authors not only contribute to the richness of the genre but also foster a more empathetic and understanding society. As contemporary romance continues to evolve, the commitment to diversity and representation will remain central to its growth, ensuring that love—in all its forms—is honored and celebrated.

Chapter 9

Character Evolution

In the heart of compelling contemporary romance lies the journey of character evolution—stories that captivate not merely through the unfolding romance but through the transformative journeys of the characters themselves. Developing characters who evolve throughout the story, learning from their experiences and changing in meaningful ways, is crucial for creating narratives that resonate deeply with readers. This evolution mirrors the complexities of real-life growth and change, making characters relatable and their stories memorable.

Character evolution in contemporary romance is about crafting a journey of self-discovery and personal growth alongside the romantic plot. This journey often begins with characters facing personal challenges, internal conflicts, or external obstacles that test their beliefs, values, and resolve. Through these trials, characters are pushed to confront their flaws, fears, and desires, setting the stage for growth. For instance, in "Eleanor Oliphant is Completely Fine" by Gail Honeyman, although not a traditional contemporary romance, Eleanor's journey towards confronting her painful past and opening herself up to the possibility of love and friendship exemplifies meaningful character evolution.

The key to effective character development is creating scenarios that challenge characters in specific, tailored ways that speak to their initial state of being. These challenges should not only be relevant to the character's personal arc but should also intertwine with the romantic elements of the story, ensuring that the evolution is both believable and deeply tied to the narrative's emotional core. Colleen Hoover's "It Ends with Us" masterfully depicts this through its protagonist, Lily, whose personal growth is inextricably linked with her romantic decisions, illustrating the complexities of love and strength.

Authentic character evolution also involves a nuanced portrayal of learning and change. Characters might take two steps forward and one step back, reflecting the often non-linear nature of personal growth. This portrayal ensures that characters' development feels realistic and earned, resonating with readers' own experiences of change. In "The Bromance Book Club" by Lyssa Kay Adams, the protagonist Gavin's efforts to save his marriage by learning from romance novels is a testament to the sometimes unconventional, yet profoundly meaningful paths to personal growth.

Moreover, supporting characters play a vital role in the protagonist's journey, serving as mirrors, challengers, or catalysts for change. These relationships are pivotal in providing the protagonist with perspective, motivation, or the necessary confrontation to spur growth. This dynamic is beautifully illustrated in "Beach Read" by Emily Henry, where the protagonists, both writers with differing views on life and love, challenge each other to confront their prejudices and past pains, leading to significant personal growth.

The culmination of character evolution in contemporary romance is often linked to the climax or resolution of the romantic plot, where characters must apply their learned lessons in a way that showcases their growth. This moment is crucial for demonstrating how the characters have changed and why they are now ready for the love they've been seeking or fighting to preserve. Such growth not only provides a satisfying conclusion to the romantic arc but also leaves readers with a sense of closure and fulfillment regarding the characters' personal journeys.

. . .

In crafting contemporary romance, the aim should be to tell stories where love acts as both a catalyst and a reward for personal growth. Developing characters who evolve meaningfully throughout the narrative ensures that the romance is not just a tale of love between two people but a journey of becoming who they need to be for themselves and each other. This approach to character development not only enriches the narrative but also elevates the genre, making contemporary romance a powerful medium for exploring the transformative power of love and personal growth.

Chapter 10

Building the Perfect Setting

The setting in contemporary romance novels is far more than just a backdrop; it's an integral component that shapes the narrative, characters, and emotional landscape of the story. Choosing and depicting modern world settings that enhance the romance and add depth to the story requires careful consideration and creativity. Whether it's the pulsating energy of a bustling city, the close-knit community of a cozy small town, or the allure of a captivating foreign locale, the setting can dramatically influence the tone, plot, and character development of the romance.

In a bustling city setting, the vibrancy and chaos of urban life provide a rich tapestry for contemporary romance. Cities like New York, London, or Tokyo are melting pots of culture, ambition, and serendipity, offering endless possibilities for chance encounters, whirlwind romances, and the challenges of maintaining love amidst the hustle. The city's landmarks, parks, and hidden gems become stages for key moments in the romance, while the pace of city life mirrors the intensity and urgency of the characters' relationship. Authors can leverage the city's diversity to introduce a wide range of supporting characters and subplots that enrich the narrative, making the setting feel like a character in its own right.

Conversely, the cozy small town setting offers a stark contrast to the urban environment. Here, the sense of community, long-standing relationships, and the slower pace of life play pivotal roles in shaping the romance. Small towns, with their traditions, local festivals, and shared history, provide a sense of belonging and identity that deeply influences the characters' journeys. Authors can use these settings to explore themes of homecoming, redemption, and the tension between longing for escape and the pull of home. The small town setting is perfect for romances that delve into the characters' backgrounds and the impact of their shared past on their present relationship.

Exploring a captivating foreign locale opens up a realm of adventure, discovery, and the excitement of the unknown. Settings like a quaint village in Italy, a beach resort in Thailand, or the rugged landscapes of New Zealand can act as catalysts for change, pushing characters out of their comfort zones and into new emotional territories. The foreign setting becomes a playground for exploration, not just of the locale but also of each other. Authors can weave in elements of cultural exploration, language barriers, and the exhilaration of travel to heighten the romance and the characters' personal growth.

The choice of setting also plays a crucial role in the development of the characters. The environment they inhabit influences their lifestyles, choices, and the obstacles they face. In a city, a character might grapple with the anonymity and isolation of urban life, while in a small town, they might struggle with the weight of expectations and gossip. In a foreign land, the challenge might lie in navigating cultural differences and finding a sense of belonging. These settings not only shape the characters but also offer unique challenges and opportunities for growth that are integral to the romance.

Moreover, the setting can act as a metaphor for the relationship itself. A bustling city might symbolize the complexity and unpredictability of love, while a small town may reflect a desire for roots and connection. A foreign locale might signify the journey of discovery that lies at the heart of falling in love. By drawing parallels between the setting and the emotional journey of the characters, authors can add depth and resonance to the story.

In depicting these settings, sensory details are key. The sights, sounds, smells, and textures of the environment should be vividly portrayed to immerse readers in the world of the story. These details not only bring the setting to life but also enhance the emotional tone of the narrative, making the romance more vivid and compelling.

Incorporating the setting into the plot and character development requires intentionality. The challenges and opportunities presented by the environment should directly impact the romance and the characters' growth. Whether it's the anonymity of a big city allowing for a fresh start, the intimacy of a small town rekindling old flames, or the adventure of a foreign locale sparking new passions, the setting should be woven seamlessly into the fabric of the story.

Ultimately, building the perfect setting in contemporary romance is about creating a world that enhances and enriches the romance at its core. By carefully choosing and depicting settings that resonate with the story's emotional journey, authors can craft narratives that captivate readers, transporting them to places where love, in all its forms, flourishes against a backdrop that is as integral to the story as the characters themselves.

Chapter 11

Realism and Research

The authenticity of the setting plays a pivotal role in grounding the story in reality and enhancing the reader's immersion. Realism in these narratives is not just a backdrop but a crucial element that influences the characters' behaviors, choices, and the overall believability of the romance. Accurate depiction of settings—be it a bustling cityscape, a serene small town, or an exotic locale—requires diligent research and a commitment to authenticity. This dedication to realism enriches the narrative, providing a solid foundation upon which the emotional journey of the characters can unfold.

The importance of accurate depiction cannot be overstated. When settings are rendered with precision and care, they lend credibility to the story, making the fictional world as convincing as the real one. This authenticity allows readers to fully engage with the narrative, suspending disbelief and investing emotionally in the characters and their journey. Conversely, inaccuracies or generalizations can jolt the reader out of the story, breaking the spell of immersion and undermining the emotional stakes of the romance. Therefore, thorough research is essential, not only to capture the essence of the setting but also to respect the experiences and realities of the people who inhabit these spaces in the real world.

Conducting research for realistic settings involves several strategies, starting with primary sources. Visiting the location in person, when possible, offers invaluable insights into the sensory details, cultural nuances, and everyday realities of the place. For authors, experiencing the setting firsthand can inspire scenes, dialogues, and character interactions that resonate with authenticity. However, when a personal visit isn't feasible, technology offers alternatives such as virtual tours, online maps, and photo archives that can provide a comprehensive sense of the place.

In addition to primary sources, engaging with secondary sources is critical for understanding the broader context of a setting. This includes reading literature, watching documentaries, and consulting academic texts about the location's history, culture, and social dynamics. Such research helps in portraying the setting with depth and complexity, avoiding stereotypes and simplistic portrayals that can detract from the story's authenticity.

Interviews and consultations with people who live in or are from the setting can offer perspectives and details that are not accessible through other means. These personal accounts can enrich the depiction of the setting with lived experiences, providing a level of authenticity that resonates with readers familiar with the place. This approach also demonstrates respect for the setting and its significance to the narrative, acknowledging that places are more than just backdrops—they are vibrant, living entities that shape and are shaped by the people who inhabit them.

Furthermore, authors should consider the temporal aspects of their settings. Cities, towns, and landscapes change over time, influenced by socio-political events, economic shifts, and cultural trends. Researching the specific time period in which the story is set ensures that the depiction of the setting is not only geographically but also historically accurate. This attention to detail supports the realism of the story, allowing the setting to serve as a true reflection of the characters' world.

Incorporating the findings from research into the narrative requires a balance. The goal is to weave factual details into the story seamlessly, enhancing the setting's authenticity without overwhelming the reader with information. The details selected should serve the story, contributing to the atmosphere, character development, and plot progression. This careful integration of research ensures that the setting enriches the romance, grounding the emotional journey of the characters in a world that feels real, vibrant, and utterly convincing.

Lastly, realism, and research are indispensable to crafting contemporary romance novels that captivate and resonate with readers. By dedicating themselves to accurate depiction and thorough research, authors can create settings that are not only authentic but also integral to the unfolding of the romance, offering readers an immersive experience that lingers long after the final page is turned.

Chapter 12

Dialogue and Banter

Contemporary dialogue and banter play a pivotal role in the fabric of contemporary romance, serving not just as a vehicle for communication but as a dynamic tool that shapes character, deepens relationships, and infuses the narrative with life. The art of crafting dialogue that resonates with the immediacy and realism of contemporary speech while also carrying the emotional weight and humor of banter requires a keen ear for how people speak and interact in real life. This element of storytelling is where the personalities of characters shine through, where tensions build, and where the chemistry between potential lovers becomes palpable. Effective dialogue captures the nuances of human communication, reflecting not just the words said but the underlying emotions, intentions, and subtext that drive interactions.

* * *

Banter serves a dual purpose. It not only entertains but also reveals the depths of characters and their relationships in a way that a straightforward narrative cannot. Through witty exchanges, playful teasing, and sharp repartee, characters can test boundaries, express affection, and engage in verbal sparring that hints at deeper feelings and connections. This lively interplay is essential in building believable, engaging relationships that captivate readers, drawing them into the dance of attraction and resistance that characterizes so much of romance. Banter can act as a form of foreplay, a verbal dance where characters negotiate their relationship, revealing vulnerabilities, insecurities, and desires. It's in these moments of shared laughter and quick-witted exchanges that the spark between characters often ignites, transforming mere dialogue into a crucial element of the romantic tension that drives the story.

* * *

Crafting contemporary dialogue and banter that feels authentic yet charged with romantic potential challenges writers to balance realism with the heightened reality of fiction. Dialogue must sound natural, mirroring the way people speak in real life, including the interruptions, hesitations, and colloquialisms that characterize actual speech. Yet, it must also serve the narrative, propelling the plot forward, deepening character development, and escalating the romantic tension. To achieve this, authors must become astute observers of real-world dialogue, tuning into the rhythms and patterns of everyday speech and then distilling these observations into dialogue that crackles with energy, emotion, and authenticity. The most memorable contemporary romances are those that manage to capture the essence of genuine human interaction, where every exchange, whether fraught with emotion or bubbling with banter, feels both utterly real and beautifully idealized, a testament to the power of words to connect, challenge, and charm.

Chapter 13

Writing Sparkling Dialogue

Writing sparkling dialogue in contemporary romance is an art form that demands a nuanced understanding of character, timing, and the delicate dance of human interaction. The dialogue must do more than simply convey information; it should breathe life into the characters, revealing their personalities, desires, and fears while advancing the plot and enriching the reader's engagement with the story. To achieve this, authors must delve deeply into their characters, understanding not just what they would say but how they would say it in a manner that reflects their unique voice and perspective. This requires a keen ear for speech patterns, regional dialects, and individual quirks, ensuring that each character's dialogue is distinct and authentic to their background, experiences, and emotional state.

One technique for crafting sparkling dialogue is to infuse it with wit and humor, elements that can elevate the text from mere conversation to a lively and engaging exchange. Wit and humor serve multiple purposes: they can diffuse tension, reveal character depth, and create moments of connection between characters. However, the key to successfully integrating these elements lies in their naturalness and relevance to the character's voice and situation. Forced humor can fall flat, so the wit must emerge organically from the characters' personalities and the dynamics of their relationship. Through playful banter, ironic observations, or light-hearted teasing, humor should enrich the dialogue in a way that feels true to the characters and their developing relationship.

Another important aspect of writing sparkling dialogue is the ability to convey the dynamics of the characters' relationship through their exchanges. Dialogue can subtly show power shifts, growing intimacy, or emerging conflict, providing readers with insight into the evolving nature of the relationship. Techniques such as interrupting, talking over each other, or finishing each other's sentences can indicate familiarity and closeness. At the same time, tone, pace, and subject matter changes can signal shifts in emotional states or relationship dynamics. By paying close attention to these subtleties, authors can use dialogue to communicate what's happening on the surface and hint at the undercurrents of emotion and tension that drive the narrative forward.

Furthermore, the strategic use of silence, or what is left unsaid, can be as powerful as the dialogue itself. Moments of silence, pauses, and hesitations can speak volumes, adding layers of meaning and emotion to the characters' interactions. These non-verbal cues invite readers to read between the lines, engaging more deeply with the characters and their internal struggles. In crafting dialogue, authors must consider the words and the spaces between them, using silence to build tension, convey unspoken feelings, or create moments of poignant understanding between characters.

Writing sparkling dialogue in contemporary romance is a complex blend of artistry, empathy, and observation. It requires a deep understanding of the characters, a sharp sense of timing, and a flair for capturing the nuances of human communication. By mastering these techniques, authors can create dialogue that entertains and deepens the readers' connection to the characters and their journey, making the romance at the heart of the story shine all the brighter.

Chapter 14

Modern Communication

Incorporating contemporary forms of communication, such as texting and social media, into the fabric of a romance narrative offers a unique opportunity to reflect the realities of modern relationships. These digital interactions have become integral to how people connect, flirt, and maintain relationships, making their inclusion in contemporary romance not just relevant but essential for authenticity. However, weaving these elements into the story in a way that feels natural and enhances the narrative demands careful consideration of pacing, character development, and plot dynamics.

With its brevity and immediacy, texting can be a powerful tool for revealing character traits, advancing the plot, and creating tension or intimacy. The key to incorporating texting effectively is ensuring it mirrors the characters' personalities and relationship stage. For example, emojis, shorthand, and inside jokes can convey a growing familiarity and affection between characters. At the same time, miscommunications and the absence of replies can heighten conflict or misunderstanding. Texting scenes should serve the narrative, providing insights into the characters' thoughts and feelings while moving the story forward. Crafting these exchanges requires a balance between realism—capturing how people genuinely text—and narrative efficiency, ensuring that each message further pushes the emotional or plot-driven envelope.

Social media adds another layer to character and relationship development, offering a public platform where private emotions and connections can be hinted at or displayed. The portrayal of social media in romance narratives can highlight the contrast between a character's online persona and their real-life vulnerabilities, adding depth to their characterization. It can also serve as a plot device, where public posts and interactions lead to jealousy, misunderstandings, or revelations that propel the romantic tension forward. However, the challenge lies in integrating social media into the story in a way that enriches rather than detracts from the primary narrative. Authors must navigate the intricacies of online communication—its performative nature, the potential for anonymity, and its impact on privacy and intimacy—ensuring that these elements enhance rather than overshadow the developing romance.

Moreover, the inclusion of modern communication must reflect the generational and cultural contexts of the characters. Younger characters might naturally gravitate towards newer platforms and use digital communication more frequently, while characters from older generations or different cultural backgrounds might interact differently online. This diversity in communication styles and preferences can add realism to the story, acknowledging the varied ways in which digital communication influences relationships today. Authors need to research and understand the nuances of how different demographics use technology to communicate, ensuring that their portrayal resonates with authenticity.

The successful integration of texting and social media into contemporary romance narratives hinges on the ability to use these tools as extensions of character and relationship development. They should provide unique insights into the characters' inner worlds, reflect the complexities of modern love, and contribute to the narrative momentum. By thoughtfully weaving these contemporary forms of communication into the story, authors can create richer, more relatable narratives that speak to the experiences of today's readers, capturing the essence of romance in the digital age.

Chapter 15

Avoiding Clichés

Avoiding clichés in dialogue is crucial for maintaining originality and engaging the reader on a deeper level. Clichés, by their very nature, are predictable and worn out from overuse, leading to a stale and uninspired narrative. To craft dialogue that feels fresh and authentic, authors must delve beyond surface-level interactions and explore their characters' unique voices and experiences. This involves a conscious effort to listen to how people speak in real life, noting the peculiarities, rhythms, and patterns that make everyday conversations distinctive and personal. By tuning into the specifics of human speech, writers can inject their dialogue with the kind of originality and nuance that elevates it above clichéd exchanges.

One effective strategy is to imbue dialogue with specific details relevant to the characters' backgrounds, interests, and current situations. This specificity not only helps avoid generic expressions but also deepens character development and enriches the story world. For instance, characters with specific hobbies, professions, or cultural backgrounds can use terminology and references unique to their experiences, making their interactions more authentic and engaging. This approach requires thorough research and an empathetic understanding of the characters' worlds, ensuring that the dialogue accurately reflects their personalities and lives. Authors can craft conversations that resonate with truth and originality by focusing on what makes each character unique.

Another key to refreshing dialogue is to embrace subtext and the power of what is left unsaid. Often, the most impactful moments in conversation come from the underlying tensions, desires, and emotions that characters are unwilling or unable to express directly. This layer of complexity adds depth to the dialogue, encouraging readers to read between the lines and engage more actively with the narrative. Crafting dialogue that hints at the unsaid requires a delicate balance, ensuring that the subtext is clear enough for readers to perceive without explicitly spelling out the characters' thoughts and feelings. This nuanced approach to dialogue avoids clichés and mirrors the complexity of real-life communication, where so much of what we feel and think is conveyed through tone, hesitation, and omission.

Revising and editing play critical roles in eliminating clichés from dialogue. The first draft of a conversation may naturally lean on familiar phrases and structures simply because they are readily accessible in the writer's mind. However, the revision process is an opportunity to critically evaluate each line of dialogue, asking whether it serves the character and the story or merely fills space with predictable language. Experimenting with different ways to express the same idea can uncover more original and impactful ways to convey the characters' thoughts and emotions. This iterative process of refinement and experimentation allows authors to hone their dialogue, stripping away clichés to reveal the fresh, compelling interactions that lie beneath.

Avoiding clichés in dialogue is essential for crafting a story that feels vibrant and true to life. By paying attention to the specifics of character and context, embracing subtext, and rigorously revising, authors can ensure that their dialogue contributes to a narrative that captivates readers with its originality and authenticity.

Chapter 16

Crafting the Meet-Cute

Crafting the meet-cute in contemporary romance is an essential skill, as it sets the tone for the relationship and injects an initial spark that captivates readers' interest from the outset. The meet-cute is more than just the first encounter between potential romantic partners; it's a pivotal moment that embodies the promise of romance, imbued with potential, humor, and a touch of destiny. To create a memorable meet-cute, authors must balance originality with the familiar warmth that fans of the genre love, ensuring that this initial meeting resonates with authenticity and intrigue. It's not merely about bringing two characters together; it's about doing so in a way that feels both inevitable and serendipitous, laying the groundwork for the emotional and narrative development that follows.

Innovation within the meet-cute scenario is key to standing out in the contemporary romance genre. While traditional meet-cutes often rely on chance encounters or a series of comedic mishaps, modern interpretations can draw on the realities of contemporary life, such as a mix-up in a coffee shop mobile order, a shared Uber pool ride gone awry, or an accidental text sent to the wrong person. These scenarios reflect how technology and modern living intersect with the quest for connection, offering a fresh take on the concept of serendipitous encounters. Moreover, integrating the characters' hobbies, professions, or passions into their meet-cute can provide depth and relevance to the encounter, making the moment feel organic to the story and meaningful to the characters' development.

To truly resonate, the meet-cute should also hint at the characters' complexities and the dynamics of their forthcoming relationship. It's an opportunity to showcase their personalities, quirks, and the initial spark of attraction that draws them together despite any differences or obstacles that may stand in their way. This requires a delicate balance of dialogue, action, and internal monologue, allowing readers to glimpse the characters' immediate reactions and the emotional undercurrents of their encounter. Whether it's through witty banter, a shared vulnerable moment, or a palpable tension, the meet-cute should leave readers eager to see how the relationship unfolds, invested in the characters' journey from their very first interaction.

Crafting the meet-cute is a creative challenge that demands a deep understanding of the characters and the story's emotional arc. By focusing on originality, relevance to modern life, and the emotional resonance of the encounter, authors can create meet-cutes that spark the romance and capture the readers' imaginations, setting the stage for a love story that feels both enchanting and utterly real.

Chapter 17

Importance of First Meetings

The first meeting between protagonists in a contemporary romance novel holds a power that extends far beyond the pages—it sets the tone for the entire narrative, establishes the chemistry between characters, and often encapsulates the romance theme. This pivotal moment, commonly known as the meet-cute, is not just a narrative device but a cornerstone upon which the emotional journey of the characters and their evolving relationship are built. Crafting a memorable first encounter is crucial because it lays the groundwork for the reader's investment in the characters' journey toward love. In this initial spark, whether it's a clash of personalities, a humorous misunderstanding, or a moment of unexpected connection, the potential for romance is ignited, captivating readers' imaginations and setting the stage for emotional and narrative development to follow.

First meetings in the contemporary romance genre cannot be overstated. These encounters often serve as a microcosm of the relationship's dynamics, offering a glimpse into the characters' personalities, their potential conflicts, and the nature of their attraction. A well-crafted meet-cute can immediately endear the characters to the reader, creating a sense of anticipation and engagement with their story. Whether the meeting is characterized by instant attraction, antagonism, or indifference, it provides a lens through which the subsequent evolution of their relationship can be viewed. This initial interaction is an opportunity for authors to showcase their characters' quirks, vulnerabilities, and desires, making the romance that unfolds not just believable but deeply rooted in the characters' unique experiences and emotional landscapes.

Furthermore, the versatility of the meet-cute allows authors to explore a wide range of tones and settings, reflecting the diversity of contemporary romance. From the lucky to the orchestrated, the comedic to the poignant, each type of first meeting offers different pathways into the narrative. A comedic meet-cute, for instance, can set the tone for a romance that balances humor with emotional depth. At the same time, a serendipitous encounter might underscore themes of fate and destiny in the characters' journey toward love. By carefully choosing the nature and context of the first meeting, authors can signal to readers the type of romance they can expect, whether it's light-hearted and fun, intense and dramatic, or somewhere in between.

The context in which the meet-cute occurs is equally important, offering a backdrop that enhances the emotional impact of the encounter. Whether it's in a bustling city street, at a quaint countryside inn, or during a disastrous blind date, the setting can amplify the significance of the meeting and enrich the narrative tapestry of the romance. It's within these carefully chosen settings that the characters' worlds collide, grounding their budding romance in a sense of place and time that adds layers of meaning to their story. The setting not only influences the dynamics of the first meeting but also becomes a character in its own right, shaping the trajectory of the characters' relationship and the challenges they face.

Ultimately, the importance of crafting a memorable first encounter lies in its ability to engage readers from the outset, laying the foundation for a romance that is as compelling as it is believable. A well-executed meet-cute resonates with the promise of what's to come, weaving together the threads of attraction, conflict, and connection that will drive the narrative forward. By considering the nature, tone, and setting of the first meeting, authors can create a pivotal moment that not only sparks the flame of romance but also captures the essence of the characters' journey toward love. In doing so, they ensure that the story that unfolds is not just a series of events but a meaningful exploration of love in its many forms, anchored by a first encounter that stays with the reader long after the last page is turned.

Chapter 18

Offering Creative Variations

The meet-cute serves as the critical juncture where potential love interests first cross paths, setting the stage for everything that follows. Given the genre's evolution and the diverse tastes of its audience, traditional meet-cutes—bumping into each other at a coffee shop or reaching for the same book in a bookstore—while still charming, require fresh twists to resonate with modern readers. Creative variations on the meet-cute can infuse a story with originality and relevance, reflecting contemporary settings and sensibilities. These innovative first encounters not only captivate readers but ensure that the romance feels grounded in today's world, seamlessly integrating into the overall plot, and enhancing the narrative's authenticity.

One innovative variation is the digital meet-cute, reflecting the significant role technology plays in modern relationships. Characters might first connect through a mistaken text message, a swipe on a dating app, or a comment thread on a social media post, setting the stage for a romance that bridges the online and offline worlds. Sally Thorne's "The Hating Game" hints at such modern interactions, albeit in a workplace setting, showcasing how digital beginnings can lead to profound real-world connections. This approach acknowledges the reality of digital communication as a starting point for many of today's relationships, offering a contemporary twist on the chance encounter that can lead to unexpected depth and complexity in the characters' connection.

Another variation is the meet-disaster, where the characters' first encounter is far from ideal, involving a minor catastrophe or embarrassing mishap. This could range from a disastrous first date set up by mutual friends, getting stuck together in an elevator during a power outage, or a calamitous misunderstanding at a social event. Christina Lauren's "Beautiful Bastard" begins with a contentious relationship between the protagonists that adds layers of tension and humor, exemplifying how a less-than-perfect start can evolve into a compelling love story. The meet-disaster plays on the adage that first impressions aren't always right, allowing for character growth and a gradual build-up of attraction that feels earned and genuine.

Incorporating a thematic meet-cute offers another variation, where the characters' first meeting directly ties into the novel's broader theme or message. For instance, if the story explores themes of environmental conservation, the protagonists might first encounter each other at a beach clean-up, a protest, or working for rival green organizations. This method not only establishes the initial connection between the characters but also sets a meaningful backdrop for their relationship to develop, weaving personal and thematic elements together seamlessly. In "The Unhoneymooners" by Christina Lauren, the protagonists find themselves on a non-honeymoon together after a wedding disaster, cleverly tying the meet-cute to themes of luck, chance, and the role of fate in love.

The interrupted meet-cute presents yet another creative variation, where the characters' first encounter is cut short, leaving both with an unfinished business or lingering curiosity about the other. This could happen due to an urgent phone call, a sudden emergency, or one character having to rush off unexpectedly, setting up a tantalizing scenario where both are left wanting more. This kind of setup not only sparks immediate interest but also creates a compelling narrative drive as the characters seek to find each other again. In "Attachments" by Rainbow Rowell, the connection initially forms through intercepted emails, an indirect form of meeting that perfectly captures the essence of an interrupted meet-cute, leaving room for curiosity and anticipation to build.

Lastly, the unforeseen reunion variation, where characters who have a shared history unexpectedly reunite after years apart, offers a rich canvas for exploring past connections and unresolved tensions. This reunion can reignite old feelings, uncover secrets, or heal past wounds, providing a deep well of emotional content to drive the story forward. "Love and Other Words" by Christina Lauren masterfully employs this variation, exploring the complexities of a rekindled romance from the protagonists' youth, demonstrating how a shared past can add depth and resonance to the romance.

These variations on the meet-cute not only reflect contemporary life but also enrich the narrative, ensuring that the romance resonates with authenticity and depth. By creatively reimagining this quintessential moment, authors can craft stories that captivate the modern reader, blending innovation with the timeless appeal of finding love in unexpected places.

Chapter 19

Adding Emotional Depth and Conflict

Emotional depth and conflict are the twin pillars that elevate contemporary romances from mere storytelling to a profound exploration of the human condition. These elements, when skillfully interwoven into the narrative, not only drive the plot but also deepen the reader's connection to the characters, making their journey toward love both compelling and believable. Emotional depth allows readers to delve into the characters' inner worlds, experiencing their fears, hopes, desires, and insecurities as if they were their own. This depth is achieved through nuanced character development, where their emotional landscapes are laid bare for the reader, fostering empathy and understanding. Conflict, on the other hand, acts as the catalyst for growth and change, challenging characters to confront their deepest fears and overcome barriers to their happiness. It is within this crucible of conflict that characters are forged, emerging as more complete individuals capable of giving and receiving love.

The essence of emotional depth lies in the authenticity with which characters' emotions are portrayed. Readers must believe in the characters' feelings, recognizing their own experiences and emotions reflected in the story. This connection is what turns a simple narrative into a mirror, showing readers aspects of themselves and offering insights into their own relationships. To achieve this, authors delve into the complexities of love, loss, joy, and pain, presenting characters who are multifaceted and real. Conflicts in these stories often stem from internal struggles—past traumas, vulnerabilities, or deeply held beliefs that hinder the characters' ability to love fully. By navigating these emotional obstacles, characters grow, and through their growth, readers are offered a window into the transformative power of love. For example, in Colleen Hoover's "It Ends with Us," the protagonist's journey through love, heartbreak, and resilience offers profound commentary on the complexities of abusive relationships, challenging readers to consider the difficult choices faced by those who experience them.

Additionally, the role of conflict cannot be overstated. Conflict introduces tension and uncertainty into the narrative, making the path to love arduous but ultimately more rewarding. It is through conflict that the stakes of the romance are raised, compelling characters to fight for their happy ending. This struggle not only adds suspense and drama to the story but also highlights the characters' strengths, weaknesses, and capacity for change. The most compelling conflicts are those that resonate on a personal level, whether they arise from external pressures like societal norms and expectations, or internal conflicts stemming from personal insecurities or miscommunications. In "Normal People" by Sally Rooney, the evolving relationship between Connell and Marianne exemplifies how deeply personal and societal conflicts can entwine, affecting their ability to maintain a stable relationship. Their story illustrates how emotional depth and conflict are intricately linked, driving the narrative forward and ensuring that their journey toward understanding and acceptance is both relatable and deeply moving.

In crafting this genre, the integration of emotional depth and conflict is essential for creating stories that not only entertain but also resonate on a deeper emotional level. These elements reflect the truth that love, in all its forms, is a journey marked by challenges and growth. By portraying this journey with honesty and sensitivity, contemporary romance offers readers not just escapism, but also a reflection on the complexities of love and the enduring hope for connection and happiness.

Chapter 20

Balancing Conflict

Balancing internal and external conflicts in contemporary romance is akin to walking a tightrope—too much weight on either side, and the narrative risks tumbling into melodrama or stagnation. A compelling romance thrives on conflict, as it's the fuel that drives the story forward, challenging characters, and testing their love. However, achieving the right equilibrium between the struggles within the characters and the challenges imposed by their environment or situation is crucial. This balance ensures that the narrative maintains tension and engagement without overwhelming readers with unrelenting obstacles or introspection that stalls the progression of the relationship.

Internal conflict often delves into the emotional and psychological barriers a character faces in pursuing or accepting love. These can stem from past traumas, fears of vulnerability, self-doubt, or deeply ingrained beliefs about worthiness and happiness. External conflict, meanwhile, introduces factors outside the characters' control that impact their relationship. These can include familial objections, societal norms, geographical distance, or professional rivalries. To balance these conflicts, authors must weave them together in a way that each informs and exacerbates the other, creating a complex web of challenges that the characters must navigate. This interplay between internal and external conflicts should feel organic, with personal growth and external resolution feeding into one another. For example, a character's fear of commitment (internal conflict) may be heightened by a job offer in another city (external conflict), forcing them to confront their fears directly.

Crafting a narrative that keeps readers invested without veering into melodrama requires a nuanced understanding of pacing and character development. Authors should aim to escalate conflicts gradually, allowing characters time to reflect, react, and grow. This pacing ensures that readers remain engaged, rooting for the characters as they tackle each obstacle. It's also important to inject moments of relief, joy, and connection between the protagonists to offer readers a respite from the tension and to highlight what's at stake. These moments of vulnerability and intimacy are crucial for deepening the emotional connection between characters (and with the reader), providing a counterbalance to the conflicts they face. By carefully timing these peaks and valleys of emotional intensity, authors can craft a narrative that resonates deeply without overwhelming the reader.

Moreover, resolving conflicts in a contemporary romance should feel earned and realistic, avoiding the temptation to tie up every loose end with a neat bow. This approach might mean that while the main conflict is resolved, some challenges remain, reflecting the complexities of real life and relationships. The resolution should stem from character growth and the choices they make, rather than deus ex machina or overly convenient plot devices. This authenticity in how conflicts are handled not only prevents the story from veering into melodrama but also reinforces the themes of resilience, hope, and the transformative power of love.

In summary, balancing internal and external conflicts in contemporary romance is a delicate art that requires careful plotting, character exploration, and an understanding of narrative pacing. By intertwining these conflicts in a way that feels natural and by pacing their escalation and resolution thoughtfully, authors can create compelling narratives that captivate readers. These stories reflect the truth that while love is seldom easy, the journey through conflict to resolution is what makes it truly rewarding.

Chapter 21

Deepening Emotional Stakes

Deepening the emotional stakes in contemporary romances is essential for creating a narrative that resonates with readers on a profound level. It's the emotional connection between characters, and between characters and readers, that transforms a story from a simple series of events into a meaningful journey of love, growth, and discovery. Achieving this depth requires a nuanced approach to character development, plot construction, and thematic exploration. One fundamental strategy is to delve into the characters' backstories and inner worlds, revealing their fears, desires, and vulnerabilities. By fully understanding who the characters are—their past traumas, their dreams for the future, and the obstacles they've overcome—authors can craft interactions and conflicts that test and reveal these aspects of their personalities. This not only adds complexity to the characters but also invites readers to invest emotionally in their journey, empathizing with their struggles and rooting for their success.

Building emotional stakes also involves crafting relationships that are rich, multifaceted, and reflective of real-life complexities. Relationships should evolve over time, shaped by experiences, conflicts, and moments of vulnerability. Authors can deepen the emotional connection by allowing characters to share personal stories, face challenges together, and support each other's growth. These shared experiences build intimacy, making the relationship feel earned and authentic. Furthermore, integrating moments where characters recognize and articulate their feelings—whether through grand gestures, quiet confessions, or acts of sacrifice—can significantly heighten the emotional stakes. These moments not only mark key points of emotional development but also create memorable scenes that resonate with readers, drawing them deeper into the romance.

Handling sensitive topics with nuance and respect is crucial for deepening emotional stakes while ensuring that the narrative remains empathetic and authentic. Whether addressing issues like mental health, trauma, or social inequalities, it's important to approach these topics with careful research, sensitivity, and an understanding of the diverse experiences of readers. This might involve consulting experts, working with sensitivity readers, or drawing on personal experiences to portray these issues accurately and thoughtfully. By treating sensitive topics with the depth and respect they deserve, authors can create stories that not only entertain but also educate and resonate on a deeper level, fostering a stronger emotional connection with readers who may see their own experiences reflected in the narrative.

Incorporating internal and external conflicts that challenge the characters' growth and relationship in meaningful ways is another strategy for deepening emotional stakes. Conflicts should stem naturally from the characters' backstories, personalities, and the world they inhabit, pushing them to confront their fears and weaknesses. As characters navigate these conflicts, they should face genuine risks and consequences, making their choices and sacrifices feel significant. This not only adds tension and drama to the narrative but also underscores the emotional stakes of the romance, making the journey toward love and happiness feel all the more rewarding.

Finally, deepening emotional stakes requires a balance between showing and telling. While it's important to articulate the characters' emotions and thoughts, showing these emotions through actions, decisions, and interactions can be even more powerful. Show how the characters' feelings influence their behavior, affect their relationships, and drive the plot forward. This approach allows readers to infer the depth of the characters' emotions, engaging their empathy and imagination. By combining thoughtful character development, careful handling of sensitive topics, meaningful conflicts, and a balance of showing and telling, authors can craft contemporary romances that not only entertain but also evoke deep emotional responses, creating a lasting impact on readers.

Chapter 22

Steamy Scenes (How Far, How Much)

The question of how far steamy scenes can go is often at the forefront of both authors' and readers' minds. This genre, known for its diversity and adaptability, offers a broad spectrum of heat levels, from sweet and closed-door to explicit and open-door encounters. The boundaries of steaminess are not fixed but fluctuate with societal norms, audience expectations, and individual authorial style. As contemporary romance continues to evolve, so too does the portrayal of intimacy, challenging authors to navigate the delicate balance between authenticity, sensitivity, and reader preferences.

The extent to which steamy scenes are incorporated into contemporary romance varies widely, influenced by the story's tone, the characters' development, and the intended audience. Some authors, like Colleen Hoover, are known for their ability to craft deeply emotional relationships with moderate heat levels, focusing on the emotional depth and connection between characters rather than explicit details. Hoover's "It Ends with Us" is a poignant example, where the emphasis is on the emotional dynamics of the relationship, offering steamy moments that are more implied than explicit, yet no less impactful.

On the other end of the spectrum, authors such as E.L. James and Sylvia Day have pushed the boundaries of steaminess in contemporary romance with their explicit content. James' "Fifty Shades of Grey" series and Day's "Crossfire" series both explore themes of desire, power, and vulnerability through detailed sexual encounters. These works, while controversial for their explicitness, have garnered massive followings and sparked conversations about the role and portrayal of sexual content in romance literature, highlighting the genre's capacity to explore complex emotional and physical landscapes.

The question of how far steamy scenes can go is also contextualized by the subgenres and themes within contemporary romance. For instance, romantic suspense or paranormal romance might incorporate steamy scenes that also serve to heighten the overall tension and drama of the narrative. In contrast, romances that tackle serious or sensitive topics might approach steaminess with more restraint, focusing on the emotional connection rather than physical details to maintain the narrative's tone and respect the subject matter.

Exceptions to the typical boundaries of steaminess often occur when authors deliberately choose to challenge genre conventions or explore specific themes that necessitate a deeper dive into physical intimacy. For example, Sierra Simone's "Priest" takes an unflinching look at desire within the confines of religious vows, using explicit scenes to explore themes of faith, guilt, and love. Simone's work exemplifies how steamy scenes can serve a narrative purpose beyond titillation, probing the depths of character psychology and societal taboos.

The increasing demand for diversity and representation in romance has also influenced how steaminess is portrayed, with more authors striving to depict a wider range of experiences, orientations, and identities. This inclusivity extends to the portrayal of intimacy, challenging authors to consider how different backgrounds and experiences affect characters' views on and experiences of desire. Helen Hoang's "The Kiss Quotient," featuring a neurodiverse protagonist and a nuanced exploration of intimacy, illustrates how steamy scenes can be crafted with sensitivity and insight, enriching the narrative and deepening character development.

Ultimately, the question of how far steamy can go in contemporary romance is one that each author must navigate based on their creative vision, audience expectations, and the specific demands of their story. The genre's flexibility and the readers' broad spectrum of preferences ensure that there is room for a wide variety of approaches to steaminess, from the sweet to the scorching. As contemporary romance continues to evolve, so too will the ways in which authors explore the complexities of desire, consent, and emotional connection, pushing boundaries and challenging conventions to tell stories that resonate with authenticity and depth.

Chapter 23

Navigating Heat Levels

Navigating heat levels in contemporary romance is akin to an art form, where the intensity and explicitness of romantic and sexual content must harmonize with the story's emotional journey, character development, and the intended audience's expectations. The spectrum of heat levels ranges broadly, from "sweet" romances, where physical intimacy is implied or occurs "off-page," to "spicy" or "erotic" romances, where sexual content is described in explicit detail. Understanding this spectrum and choosing the right level for a story is crucial for authors to ensure that the romance resonates authentically with readers while staying true to the narrative's tone and themes.

Sweet romances focus on the emotional connection and the build-up of romantic tension between characters, often culminating in a kiss or a declaration of love without delving into the details of physical intimacy. This approach appeals to readers who prefer to leave more to the imagination or who are drawn to the emotional aspects of a relationship rather than the physical. Sweet romances, such as those by authors like Debbie Macomber or Becky Wade, emphasize the characters' emotional journey towards love, highlighting the significance of mutual respect, understanding, and emotional support in building a lasting relationship.

Moving along the spectrum, "warm" romances introduce a moderate level of steaminess, where sexual encounters are acknowledged and may be briefly described, but not in explicit detail. This middle ground allows for a deeper exploration of the characters' physical connection while maintaining a focus on the emotional depth of the relationship. Warm romances cater to readers who appreciate a balance between the emotional and physical aspects of love without the narrative focus shifting predominantly to sexual content.

"Hot" romances turn up the heat further, offering detailed descriptions of sexual encounters between characters. These scenes are integral to the development of the relationship, serving to deepen the emotional connection and highlight the characters' compatibility, vulnerabilities, and growth. Authors like Jennifer L. Armentrout and Christina Lauren excel in this category, crafting steamy scenes that complement the emotional narrative without overshadowing it, ensuring that the physical intimacy adds to the characters' love story in meaningful ways.

At the spicier end of the spectrum, "erotic" romances prioritize the physical aspects of the relationship, with explicit sexual content serving as a central element of the story. This level of steaminess requires a delicate balance to ensure that the sexual encounters drive character development and emotional growth, rather than simply providing titillation. Works by authors such as E.L. James and Sylvia Day exemplify this category, exploring themes of desire, power dynamics, and emotional healing through detailed, explicit sexual content.

Choosing the right heat level for a story involves considering several factors, including the author's personal comfort and style, the narrative's tone and themes, and the target audience's expectations. Authors must also be mindful of the genre conventions within contemporary romance, as certain subgenres or reader demographics may have prevailing preferences regarding heat levels. Understanding and respecting these preferences can help authors connect more effectively with their readers, providing a satisfying romantic experience that aligns with audience expectations.

Incorporating the chosen heat level into a story requires a thoughtful approach to character development and plot progression. Regardless of the level of steaminess, sexual encounters should always serve to advance the narrative or deepen the characters' relationship in some way. This might involve using these moments to reveal vulnerabilities, resolve conflicts, or express the characters' emotional growth and commitment to each other. Successful integration of steamy scenes, therefore, hinges on their relevance to the story and their contribution to the overarching journey of love and self-discovery that defines the contemporary romance genre.

Moreover, navigating heat levels with sensitivity and respect for the characters and the audience is paramount. This includes ensuring that all romantic and sexual interactions are consensual, empowering, and portrayed with authenticity and care. By doing so, authors can create steamy scenes that resonate with emotional truth and enhance the narrative, regardless of where they fall on the spectrum of heat levels.

Ultimately, the choice of heat level in contemporary romance is a strategic decision that can significantly impact the story's appeal and effectiveness. By carefully considering the narrative needs, character development, and audience expectations, authors can select the appropriate level of steaminess to enrich their romance, ensuring that the physical aspects of the characters' relationship complement and deepen the emotional journey at the heart of the story.

How far can it go without ending up being Erotic?

In contemporary romances, navigating the delicate line between steamy or spicy content and crossing into the realm of erotic fiction is a nuanced art. This boundary is defined not just by the explicitness of the scenes but by how these moments are integrated into the narrative and character development. A steamy contemporary romance can push the boundaries of heat levels, offering readers a vivid exploration of physical and emotional intimacy without necessarily venturing into the domain of erotic literature. The distinction often lies in the purpose and depth of the sexual content and its role in advancing the story or deepening the emotional connection between characters.

Steamy or spicy contemporary romances focus on building a deep emotional connection between the characters, with physical intimacy serving as an expression of this growing bond. The key is ensuring that these steamy scenes are rooted in the development of the relationship, revealing vulnerabilities, strengthening emotional ties, and propelling the characters' journey forward. For example, in "The Hating Game" by Sally Thorne, the physical encounters between the protagonists are charged with emotional depth, serving as a culmination of their evolving relationship from antagonists to lovers. The steaminess in Thorne's narrative enhances the emotional stakes without relying on explicit content as the primary driver of the relationship, maintaining a balance that keeps the story within the contemporary romance genre.

Contrastingly, erotic fiction often places a greater emphasis on the sexual aspects of the relationship, with the plot and character development sometimes taking a secondary role to the exploration of physical desire and sexual discovery. While contemporary romance might explore similar themes of desire and intimacy, the distinction lies in the narrative's focus. A contemporary romance like "Beautiful Disaster" by Jamie McGuire, though undeniably steamy, prioritizes the emotional turmoil and personal growth of the characters alongside their physical attraction, ensuring that the romance remains the core of the narrative.

The inclusion of steamy scenes in contemporary romance also hinges on the author's skill in weaving these moments into the fabric of the story seamlessly. The challenge is to portray sexual content in a way that feels organic to the characters' development, rather than gratuitous or out of place. Julie James' "Practice Makes Perfect," for instance, strikes a balance by building sexual tension and desire as integral components of the protagonists' competitive relationship, culminating in moments of physical intimacy that feel earned and essential to their emotional reconciliation. This approach maintains the steaminess without overshadowing the narrative's romantic and personal growth aspects.

Audience expectations also play a crucial role in defining how far a steamy contemporary romance can go. Readers of contemporary romance are often looking for stories that, while possibly including explicit scenes, primarily explore the complexities of relationships, emotional growth, and the journey to love. Authors like Helen Hoang, with books such as "The Kiss Quotient," manage to explore deep emotional connections and issues of identity and vulnerability, all while including steamy scenes that complement but do not dominate the narrative. Hoang's work exemplifies how contemporary romance can address issues of personal and sexual exploration without tipping fully into erotica.

Finally, the distinction between steamy contemporary romance and erotica can also be navigated through the use of language and perspective. In contemporary romance, the language used to describe steamy scenes often focuses on the emotional experience and the sensory aspects of intimacy rather than explicit details. The perspective is usually deeply tied to the characters' emotional states, ensuring that readers are invested in the characters' internal experiences as much as the physical ones. This careful choice of language and focus ensures that even when contemporary romances venture into spicy territory, they retain a strong emotional core that distinguishes them from erotica.

In summary, steamy contemporary romances can explore the depths of desire and intimacy without crossing into erotic fiction by focusing on emotional development, ensuring that physical scenes enhance the narrative, and maintaining a balance that aligns with readers' expectations for the genre. Through skilled storytelling and a deep understanding of the characters' emotional journeys, authors can craft narratives that are both sensually rich and emotionally resonant, offering readers a compelling exploration of love and intimacy within the framework of the genre.

Chapter 24

Balancing Physical Attraction with Emotional Development

Balancing physical attraction with emotional development is crucial for creating a compelling narrative that resonates with readers on multiple levels. This delicate equilibrium ensures that the relationship between the characters is not solely predicated on physical desire but is enriched by a deep, emotional connection that evolves over the course of the story. Physical attraction often serves as the initial spark that draws characters together, but it is the emotional development that transforms this spark into a lasting flame. To achieve this balance, authors must craft scenes and interactions that reveal the characters' vulnerabilities, hopes, fears, and dreams, allowing readers to understand and empathize with them. As characters navigate the challenges and conflicts that arise in the story, their emotional bonds are tested and strengthened, creating a multidimensional relationship that is both believable and engaging.

The journey of emotional development often involves characters learning to communicate openly, overcome personal obstacles, and support each other's growth. These elements are key to building a deeper bond that transcends physical attraction. For instance, when characters share their past hurts or future aspirations, they are offering more than just information; they are extending trust and inviting intimacy on a psychological and emotional level. This progression from attraction to emotional intimacy requires patience and timing in the narrative, ensuring that each step in the characters' relationship feels earned and authentic. The development of this bond is what ultimately convinces readers of the characters' compatibility and the durability of their love, making the eventual culmination of their physical and emotional journey together both satisfying and meaningful.

Furthermore, balancing physical attraction with emotional development allows authors to explore the theme of love as a transformative force. Through their relationship, characters can inspire each other to confront their fears, heal from past wounds, and pursue their dreams, illustrating how love can catalyze personal growth and self-discovery. This theme resonates deeply with readers, who see in these stories a reflection of love's power to change lives for the better. It also elevates the romance from a simple love story to a narrative about human resilience, connection, and the courage to be vulnerable. In doing so, contemporary romance novels offer more than just escapism; they provide insight into the complexities of love and the myriad ways it can manifest, enriching readers' understanding of relationships and the human heart.

Chapter 25

The Role of Characters & Relationship Building

Secondary characters play an indispensable role in enriching the narrative, providing depth, and facilitating the protagonists' journey towards love. These characters—be it family, friends, or antagonists—add layers of complexity, humor, and realism, creating a multidimensional story that resonates deeply with readers. By examining modern contemporary romance bestsellers, we can observe how effectively secondary characters are utilized to enhance the storytelling, offer alternative perspectives, and drive the emotional growth of the protagonists.

Take, for instance, *"Red, White & Royal Blue"* by Casey McQuiston, where secondary characters such as family members and political figures play crucial roles in shaping the protagonists' worldviews and choices. These characters not only contribute to the external pressures faced by the main characters but also provide support and comedic relief, creating a rich backdrop against which the central romance unfolds. The interactions with these secondary characters bring to light the protagonists' vulnerabilities and strengths, making their journey towards acceptance and love all the more compelling.

In Sally Rooney's *"Normal People,"* the secondary characters, including friends and family members, serve to highlight the protagonists' evolving identities and the social dynamics that influence their relationship. These characters mirror the complexities of real-life relationships, where external influences and internal struggles intertwine, affecting the course of love. Rooney masterfully uses these characters to explore themes of class, mental health, and the impact of societal expectations on personal relationships, adding a profound layer of depth to the narrative.

Talia Hibbert's *"Get a Life, Chloe Brown"* showcases secondary characters that not only bring humor and warmth to the story but also challenge the protagonists to confront their fears and misconceptions. The family dynamics and interactions with neighbors and friends enrich the storyline, offering insights into Chloe's and Red's characters. These relationships underscore the themes of personal growth, vulnerability, and the power of community, making the protagonists' journey towards love and self-acceptance more nuanced and relatable.

In, *"The Flatshare"* by Beth O'Leary provides a unique take on how secondary characters can influence the narrative without having a physical presence. Through notes and shared living spaces, the protagonists interact with each other's friends and ex-partners, revealing their personalities, fears, and desires. This novel approach highlights the importance of communication and understanding in building a relationship, showcasing how secondary characters can serve as catalysts for change, even from the sidelines.

Lastly, *"The Bride Test"* by Helen Hoang illustrates how secondary characters, particularly family members, can add layers of cultural richness and emotional complexity to the romance. Through these characters, the story explores themes of immigration, cultural differences, and the universal search for love and belonging. The family's involvement in the protagonists' relationship challenges and ultimately strengthens their bond, emphasizing the intersection of love, family, and identity.

These examples from these bestsellers underscore the versatility and significance of secondary characters in enriching the narrative. Whether through direct interaction or as part of the broader social and cultural context, these characters deepen the emotional resonance of the story, challenge the protagonists in meaningful ways, and provide additional layers of conflict and companionship. By thoughtfully integrating secondary characters, authors can craft stories that are not only about the journey of two people falling in love but also about the broader human experience, resonating with readers long after the final page is turned.

In contemporary romance, the portrayal of a variety of relationships outside the central love story is essential for creating a narrative that mirrors the complexity and richness of real life. These relationships—whether they be familial ties, friendships, professional associations, or even rivalries — serve to deepen the reader's understanding of the protagonists, providing context and contrast to the central romance. By showcasing a spectrum of interactions, authors can offer a more nuanced and comprehensive exploration of their characters, making them feel like living, breathing individuals with lives that extend beyond their romantic encounters. This multiplicity of relationships enriches the narrative, adding layers of conflict, support, and growth opportunities for the characters, ultimately enhancing the reader's engagement and investment in the story.

Familial relationships, for instance, play a crucial role in shaping characters' beliefs, values, and attitudes toward love and commitment. The dynamics within a family—from parental expectations to sibling rivalries—can significantly influence a character's approach to their romantic life, providing obstacles or encouragement. In "The Seven

Husbands of Evelyn Hugo" by Taylor Jenkins Reid, the complex familial relationships and friendships of the protagonist not only illuminate her motivations and vulnerabilities but also offer poignant insights into the sacrifices and compromises she makes in pursuit of love and success. These non-romantic relationships are instrumental in developing a rich, multidimensional character whose pursuit of love is as compelling as it is complicated.

Friendships, both old and new, offer another avenue for exploring the multifaceted nature of human connections. Friends can act as confidantes, advisors, and sources of unconditional support, but they can also introduce challenges and conflicts that test the protagonist's loyalty and priorities. In "Beach Read" by Emily Henry, the protagonists' friendships play a vital role in their emotional journeys, offering moments of levity, wisdom, and introspection that enrich the central romance. These friendships provide a backdrop against which the protagonists' growth and self-discovery are highlighted, emphasizing the importance of platonic love in one's life.

Professional relationships in contemporary romance can also add depth to the narrative, revealing aspects of the characters' ambitions, ethics, and personalities. Colleagues, mentors, and rivals introduce challenges that force characters to confront their professional aspirations and personal values, often blurring the lines between their work and personal lives. For example, in "The Hating Game" by Sally

Thorne, the protagonists' professional rivalry and mutual ambition serve as both a source of conflict and a catalyst for their evolving relationship. This interplay between their work and romantic lives adds a compelling layer of complexity to the story, making their journey toward love all the more satisfying.

The portrayal of diverse types of relationships reflects the reality of human social life, where interactions are varied and complex. In "Normal People" by Sally Rooney, the protagonists navigate a web of relationships that influence their understanding of love, identity, and belonging. These connections, fraught with miscommunications and societal pressures, not only affect their romance but also offer a broader commentary on the nature of human connections in the modern age. The novel's exploration of these varied relationships underscores the interconnectedness of love and life, highlighting the impact of social dynamics on personal growth and romantic choices.

Incorporating a variety of relationships outside the central romance also allows authors to tackle broader themes and issues, from societal norms and cultural expectations to personal identity and mental health. These themes are often explored through the protagonists' interactions with others, providing a richer context for their decisions and actions within the romantic narrative. By doing so, contemporary romance novels can transcend the bound aries of the genre, offering readers not only a compelling love story but also a reflective examination of the human condition.

Showcasing a variety of relationships outside the central romance enriches contemporary romance novels, making them more relatable, engaging, and reflective of the complexity of real life. Through these diverse interactions, characters are fully realized, themes are more deeply explored, and the central romance is grounded in a world that mirrors our own, imbued with all the challenges, joys, and intricacies of human connection.

Chapter 26

Modern Challenges

As you plot your journey of crafting a contemporary romance novel, it's essential to weave social, cultural, and personal challenges into your narrative in a way that resonates deeply with your readers. Your goal is to create a story that mirrors the complexities of the world we live in, offering not just an escape, but also insights and reflections that linger long after the last page is turned. This task, while rewarding, requires a careful balance to ensure these elements enhance rather than overshadow the romance at the heart of your story.

Begin by embedding these challenges within the fabric of your characters' lives. Make their struggles and triumphs a natural extension of the plot, allowing readers to see how these issues impact their journey toward love. For example, consider how *"The Kiss Quotient"* by Helen Hoang integrates the protagonist's autism spectrum disorder into her character development and romance. This approach ensures the story remains authentic and engaging, providing a nuanced exploration of neurodiversity.

When tackling themes such as racial diversity, LGBTQ+ rights, mental health, or environmental concerns, it's crucial to approach them with authenticity. Your narrative should reflect thorough research and, when possible, personal experiences or consultations with individuals familiar with the issues at hand. Colleen Hoover's *"It Ends with Us"* is a poignant example, addressing domestic violence with honesty and empathy, illustrating the profound effect personal challenges can have on romantic relationships.

Creating complex characters is key to capturing the nuanced realities of modern life. Your characters should embody a broad spectrum of experiences, backgrounds, and perspectives, challenging stereotypes and defying easy categorizations. Through characters who defy traditional norms—such as those in Casey McQuiston's *"Red, White & Royal Blue"*—you can enrich your romance with layers of personal and societal challenges that resonate with contemporary issues.

To avoid stereotypes, focus on portraying your characters with depth and individuality. Recognize that every person's experience is unique, and avoid simplifying or diminishing these experiences through one-dimensional portrayals.

Instead, explore your characters' varied identities, struggles, and aspirations. *"Americanah"* by Chimamanda Ngozi Adichie, while not strictly a romance, beautifully illustrates the richness of narrative that comes from treating characters as fully realized individuals, offering insightful commentary on race, immigration, and identity.

Incorporating modern challenges into your story offers you an opportunity to engage with the world in its full complexity. This doesn't mean letting these elements dominate your narrative but integrating them in a way that adds depth to your love story. The romance itself can become a beacon of hope, demonstrating how individuals navigate and surmount obstacles together. This approach not only captivates your readers but also may inspire and influence their perspectives on significant issues.

As you weave these themes and challenges into your narrative, remember to balance them carefully with the romantic elements. Your primary aim is to tell a love story that feels real and relevant. This means ensuring that the social and personal issues your characters face are integral to their development and the evolution of their relationship, rather than mere backdrops or afterthoughts.

Your role as a contemporary romance author is not just to entertain but to illuminate and challenge, to celebrate the diversity and complexity of our world through the lens of romance. By thoughtfully integrating contemporary challenges into your stories, you contribute to a genre that reflects the joys, sorrows, and resilience of the human spirit.

This journey requires empathy, patience, and a willingness to delve into the heart of human experiences. As you craft your narrative, let your characters lead the way. Allow their voices to guide you in exploring the themes that matter most to them, and in turn, to your readers. This authentic approach will not only enrich your story but also ensure that it resonates with a wide audience, making your novel not just a tale of love but a reflection on the power of connection in overcoming adversity.

Ultimately, your romance novel has the potential to be more than just a story of two people falling in love. It can be a window into the realities of life, offering hope, understanding, and empathy. By embracing the complexity of modern challenges and themes, and by creating characters that are as diverse and multifaceted as the world around us, you have the power to craft a narrative that not only entertains but also enlightens and inspires. This is the true beauty of contemporary romance: its ability to capture the essence of our times while reminding us of the enduring power of love.

Chapter 27

The Will-They-Won't-They Dynamic

The *"Will-They-Won't-They"* dynamic, a staple of the contemporary romance genre, captivates readers with the tantalizing dance of uncertainty and longing that defines the protagonists' journey towards love. This narrative device thrives on the tension and anticipation built around the potential romantic union of two characters, keeping readers hooked on every twist and turn of their relationship. The allure of this dynamic lies in its ability to mimic the complexities and unpredictabilities of real-life romance, where the path to love is rarely straightforward. It's the uncertainty, the push and pull between the characters, that fuels the emotional investment of readers, compelling them to turn page after page in hope and suspense.

Crafting a successful *"Will-They-Won't-They"* storyline requires a delicate balance between keeping the romantic tension believable and maintaining reader interest over time. The key is to develop multi-dimensional characters whose motivations, fears, and desires logically justify the fluctuating nature of their relationship. These characters must be relatable and compelling, with personal growth arcs that intersect and diverge in ways that naturally create conflict and chemistry. For example, in Sally Thorne's "The Hating Game," the protagonists' professional rivalry and personal animosities lay the groundwork for a captivating push-pull dynamic that gradually evolves into mutual respect and attraction, exemplifying how well-crafted character development can sustain the "Will-They-Won't-They" tension.

Moreover, the environment and secondary characters play pivotal roles in enriching the central dynamic. By placing the protagonists in settings or situations that force them to confront their feelings while navigating external pressures, authors can add layers of complexity to the relationship. Secondary characters, whether as allies or obstacles, can also influence the protagonists' decisions and perceptions, providing external viewpoints that challenge or reinforce the central dynamic. This interplay between the main and supporting elements of the narrative ensures that the tension remains dynamic and multifaceted, mirroring the unpredictability of love.

However, authors must navigate this dynamic with care to avoid frustrating readers with excessive obstacles or unnecessary misunderstandings that stall the relationship indefinitely. The key is to ensure that each twist in the relationship feels earned and contributes to the characters' emotional growth, rather than serving as mere plot devices to prolong the tension. This approach keeps the storyline engaging and ensures that when the characters finally confront their feelings, the resolution feels satisfying and true to their journey.

Chapter 28

Maintaining Romantic Tension

To keep the flame of romantic tension alive throughout a contemporary romance story, authors must masterfully juggle a mix of elements that keep readers on the edge of their seats. A prime method for achieving this is the adept introduction of both external and internal obstacles that resonate deeply with the characters' personal journeys. For instance, in *"The Light We Lost"* by Jill Santopolo, the lovers face life's unpredictabilities and the choices that pull them in different directions, exemplifying how real-world challenges can fuel the tension and desire between characters. Such obstacles not only sustain the narrative's momentum but also add depth to the love story, making the readers' emotional investment in the outcome even greater.

Miscommunications and misunderstandings can serve as a rich source of romantic tension, provided they stem from well-drawn character traits and past experiences. In *"One Day in December"* by Josie Silver, missed opportunities and the protagonists' misinterpretations of each other's actions create a tantalizing tension that drives the narrative. This novel showcases how effectively leveraging characters' internal conflicts and fears can lead to misunderstandings that feel both inevitable and heart-wrenchingly authentic, keeping readers hooked on the unfolding drama.

The inclusion of secondary characters and parallel story-lines can significantly amplify the main romantic tension. For example, *"Evvie Drake Starts Over"* by Linda Holmes introduces characters dealing with grief and new beginnings, which not only enriches the narrative but also mirrors and complicates the protagonists' emotional journey. These additional layers of conflict and companionship provided by secondary characters add complexity to the main romance, offering alternative perspectives and challenges that keep the reader engaged and the narrative dynamic.

Pacing plays a crucial role in maintaining tension, with the story's rhythm needing to reflect the natural progression of the relationship. In *"Beach Read"* by Emily Henry, the pacing skillfully alternates between moments of intense connection and conflict, illustrating how the timing of these interactions can heighten anticipation and deepen the emotional stakes. This deliberate pacing ensures that the narrative captures the unpredictable, often messy rhythm of real-life romance, keeping readers invested in the characters' evolving relationship.

Utilizing a dual perspective can deepen the romantic tension by allowing readers inside the minds of both protagonists, offering a dual-sided view of the longing and misunderstandings that drive the narrative. In *"Love and Other Words"* by Christina Lauren, the alternating viewpoints provide a profound insight into the characters' past and present feelings, magnifying the tension and making the moments of connection all the more impactful. This technique enriches the narrative by showing how each character grapples with their emotions, making the tension more palpable and the readers more empathetic.

The setting and atmosphere can underscore and elevate the romantic tension. In *"The Night Circus"* by Erin Morgenstern, the enchanting and mysterious backdrop of the circus acts as a catalyst for the protagonists' romance, weaving magic and mystery into their relationship. The setting not only adds an atmospheric tension but also parallels the characters' magical, fraught journey towards each other, demonstrating how the right backdrop can magnify the emotional intensity of the romance.

In weaving these elements together—obstacles, misunderstandings, secondary characters, pacing, perspective, and setting—authors can craft a contemporary romance that pulses with tension and desire. This careful construction ensures that the journey to love remains compelling, complex, and ultimately satisfying, reflecting the nuanced dance of real-life romance.

Chapter 29

Humor – Yes, use humor!

The infusion of humor is a strategic narrative choice that significantly enhances the reader's engagement and connection with the story. Humor serves as a universal language, bridging gaps between characters and readers alike, making the story more accessible and relatable. Its importance cannot be overstated, as it not only provides levity in moments of tension but also reveals the characters' personalities in a way that deepens the audience's understanding and empathy. Through witty banter, comedic situations, or the characters' internal monologues, humor acts as a lens through which the nuances of relationships and individual quirks are magnified, adding layers of depth to the narrative.

Integrating humor into a romance novel does more than just entertain; it serves as a tool for character development. Characters who use humor, whether through sarcasm, self-deprecation, or playful teasing, often appear more multi-dimensional and relatable. This use of humor can be a defense mechanism, a way to cope with nervousness, or simply a trait that endears them to others, including the reader. For instance, characters might use humor to navigate awkward first encounters or diffuse potentially confrontational situations, showcasing their quick wit and ability to adapt to the complexities of human interactions. These moments not only provide comic relief but also offer insights into the characters' thought processes and emotional resilience.

Furthermore, humor plays a critical role in deepening character relationships within the story. When characters share a sense of humor, it creates a bond that transcends the page, making their connection feel genuine and earned. This shared laughter becomes a private language, a way of communicating affection, understanding, and solidarity. It's in these moments of shared amusement that the characters' compatibility shines, illustrating how humor can be a foundation upon which deeper feelings are built. The ability to laugh together, especially in moments of adversity, underscores the strength of their bond, making the romance all the more convincing and compelling to the reader.

Humor also serves as an effective tool for lightening moments of tension, providing a release valve for both characters and readers. In the rollercoaster of emotions that characterizes contemporary romance, humor offers a moment of reprieve, a chance to catch one's breath before diving back into the drama. This balancing act ensures that the narrative maintains a dynamic rhythm, oscillating between moments of intensity and lightheartedness. Such strategic use of humor can transform potentially overwhelming scenes into manageable, even endearing, moments, allowing for a pacing that keeps the readers engaged without overwhelming them with constant high stakes or emotional turmoil.

Moreover, the use of humor in a romance novel can challenge and subvert genre conventions, offering fresh perspectives on love and relationships. By employing comedic elements, authors can tackle serious themes with a light touch, making the narrative more palatable and impactful. Humor has the power to disarm, opening up spaces for critical conversations about love, loss, identity, and societal norms in a way that is accessible and thought-provoking. This not only broadens the appeal of the story but also enriches the genre as a whole, proving that romance novels can be both profoundly meaningful and delightfully entertaining.

* * *

The role of humor extends beyond the characters and their interactions, influencing the reader's experience of the story. Laughter, even in the context of a fictional narrative, has a tangible effect on the reader, creating a sense of joy and wellbeing that enhances their engagement with the story. As readers navigate the ups and downs of the plot, humor acts as a constant, a reminder of the joy that can be found even in the most tumultuous of romances. This emotional engagement fosters a deeper connection with the story, making the characters' journey toward a happy ending all the more satisfying.

For example, Penny Reid uses humor to great effect in her *"Knitting in the City"* series, where quirky characters and witty dialogue illuminate the complexities of romantic and platonic relationships. Reid's unique blend of humor and heart showcases how laughter can deepen connections between characters, making their eventual romantic unions feel both inevitable and deeply satisfying. Her ability to weave scientific references and intellectual banter into her narratives not only entertains but also highlights the intelligence and individuality of her characters.

Sophie Kinsella, renowned for her *"Shopaholic"* series, exemplifies how humor can lighten moments of tension and add layers of depth to the romantic journey. Kinsella's protagonist, *Becky Bloomwood,* often finds herself in hilariously untenable situations, yet it's her optimistic resilience and humorous outlook on life that endear her to both the other characters and the readers. Kinsella skillfully uses humor as a tool to explore themes of consumerism, ambition, and the search for identity, all while maintaining a light-hearted tone that keeps readers hooked and hopeful for Becky's happy ending.

Helen Hoang's *"The Kiss Quotient"* and *"The Bride Test"* bring humor into the realm of contemporary romance through characters who defy conventional expectations, including those with autism spectrum disorder. Hoang's characters navigate the complexities of relationships with a refreshing honesty and humor that breaks down barriers and challenges stereotypes. The humor in Hoang's work not only provides levity but also serves to highlight the characters' growth and the genuine, heartfelt connections they form, demonstrating how humor can be both inclusive and insightful.

In *"You Deserve Each Other"* by Sarah Hogle, humor is used to explore the rejuvenation of a relationship on the brink of collapse. Hogle crafts a series of comedic yet poignant mishaps that force her protagonists to confront the realities of their pending marriage. The humor here acts as a catalyst for introspection and communication, transforming their antagonistic pranks into moments of vulnerability and reconnection. This novel showcases how humor can transform and rekindle love, even in its most challenging moments, making the journey toward a happy ending as hilarious as it is heartwarming.

Mariana Zapata's slow-burn romances, such as *"The Wall of Winnipeg and Me,"* often feature humor as a subtle but powerful tool for character development and relationship building. Zapata's protagonists typically find themselves in situations where humor emerges as a natural response to the absurdities of life, serving as a bridge between characters who might, on the surface, seem incompatible. The gradual buildup of their relationships, punctuated by moments of laughter and lighthearted banter, allows for a deep, emotional connection to form, underscoring the role of humor in developing believable, endearing romances.

"The Hating Game" by Sally Thorne is a masterclass in using humor to maintain romantic tension. The protagonists' witty exchanges and competitive antics not only drive the narrative forward but also reveal the depth of their attraction and affection for each other. Thorne demonstrates that humor, when intertwined with desire and rivalry, can create a dynamic and captivating romance that keeps readers engaged from start to finish.

Weaving humor into a contemporary romance narrative in a manner that feels both natural and story-enhancing, without detracting from the emotional depth, is a nuanced skill that can significantly elevate the reading experience. Here are some tips for incorporating humor effectively:

Understand Your Characters: Humor should stem naturally from your characters' personalities, backgrounds, and the situations they find themselves in. Create characters with unique quirks or perspectives that lend themselves to humorous observations or reactions. Understanding the nuances of your characters allows for the creation of humor that feels authentic and tailored to their experiences.

Use Dialogue Wisely: One of the most effective vehicles for humor is dialogue. Witty banter, playful teasing, or sarcastic remarks can reveal the chemistry between characters, making their interactions more dynamic and engaging. However, it's crucial to ensure that the humor arises organically from the conversation and fits the characters' relationship and the scene's context.

Incorporate Situational Humor: Situational humor, arising from the plot or setting, can add a layer of entertainment without detracting from the story's emotional core. Whether it's a series of unfortunate events or a comedic misunderstanding, situational humor should challenge your characters in a way that contributes to their growth or the evolution of their relationship.

Balance with Emotional Depth: While humor can lighten the narrative, it's important to balance it with moments of emotional depth. This balance ensures that the humor does not overshadow the story's heart but rather complements it. Use humor to break tension or offer relief after intense scenes, but always bring the focus back to the characters' emotional journey.

Subvert Expectations: Playing with genre tropes or character stereotypes in a humorous way can delight and surprise readers. By subverting expectations through humor, you can offer a fresh take on familiar scenarios, making your story stand out. This approach not only entertains but also invites readers to engage with the narrative on a deeper level.

Mind the Pacing: The pacing of humor within the narrative is crucial. Introduce humorous elements at moments that can naturally benefit from levity, using them to pace the story and keep readers engaged. However, be cautious not to overload intense or pivotal scenes with humor, as this can undermine their significance.

Respect the Emotional Journey: Ensure that the use of humor respects the characters' emotional journeys. Humor should never minimize the characters' feelings or experiences. Instead, it can be used to reveal vulnerabilities, build intimacy, or offer characters (and readers) a momentary respite from conflict.

Feedback is Key: Test the humor in your narrative with beta readers or writing groups. Humor can be subjective, and what resonates with one reader may not with another. Feedback can help you gauge whether the humor feels natural and enhances the story without undermining its emotional depth.

Incorporating humor into your contemporary romance narrative requires a thoughtful approach that respects the characters and their journeys. When done well, humor not only entertains but also deepens the readers' connection to the story, making the romance all the more satisfying and memorable.

Chapter 30

Marketing and Branding

In the ever-evolving landscape of contemporary romance, mastering the art of marketing and branding is as crucial as the craft of writing itself. For authors, distinguishing their work in a crowded market is not just about selling books; it's about establishing a connection with readers and building a loyal community around their stories. The journey begins with the understanding that branding goes beyond a consistent aesthetic or genre—it encapsulates everything from the author's voice, themes, and values to the types of stories they choose to tell. This initial step of self-discovery and positioning is fundamental. It involves a deep dive into what sets your work apart, the unique lens through which you explore the themes of love, growth, and resilience that resonate with your audience. This chapter aims to unravel the complexities of marketing and branding, offering a blueprint for authors to navigate this essential aspect of their writing career with confidence and creativity.

The modern-day digital age movement has transformed how authors connect with their audience, making an online presence an indispensable tool for marketing and branding. From social media platforms to author websites, the opportunities for engagement are boundless. However, navigating this digital terrain requires a strategic approach. Authors must curate content that reflects their brand identity, speaks to their target audience, and fosters a sense of community. Whether through behind-the-scenes glimpses into the writing process, interactive discussions about character development, or sharing personal insights that align with the themes of their books, the goal is to create a cohesive online persona that encapsulates the essence of their brand. This digital engagement not only helps build anticipation for upcoming releases but also maintains interest between publications, keeping the readership engaged and invested.

Beyond the virtual world, understanding the nuances of book marketing—from cover design and blurb crafting to choosing the right platforms for promotion—is pivotal. The cover is often the first point of contact between the book and potential readers, making its alignment with the brand's visual identity and the story's mood essential. Similarly, the blurb should capture the essence of the narrative in a way that entices readers while reflecting the author's unique voice. Effective marketing strategies also extend to choosing the right promotional channels that reach the target audience, whether through targeted ads, email newsletters, or collaborations with bloggers and other authors. Balancing these elements with authenticity and a clear understanding of the brand can turn the daunting task of marketing into an opportunity to further solidify the author's presence in the genre.

Chapter 31

Finding your Niche in Romance's Crowded Market

Finding your niche within the contemporary market is akin to discovering a secret garden where your creativity can flourish. As an experienced author, I've learned that this journey begins with introspection. Reflect on the stories that stir your soul—are you captivated by the sweetness of small-town romances like those in Robyn Carr's *"Virgin River"* series, or do you find your heart racing with the high stakes of romantic suspense akin to Lori Foster's work? Your unique voice might resonate with tales of second chances, a trope that offers endless possibilities for depth and redemption, much like in *"It Ends with Us"* by Colleen Hoover.

Dive deep into the genre, not just as a reader but as a researcher. Pay attention to the sub-genres that pique your interest. Perhaps you're drawn to the playful banter and slow-burn romance in Sally Thorne's *"The Hating Game,"* indicating a penchant for enemies-to-lovers stories. Or maybe the intricate dance of love and technology in Christina Lauren's *"My Favorite Half-Night Stand"* suggests a connection to online love tropes. This exploration is crucial; it helps identify what you enjoy writing and what resonates with readers, guiding you to a niche that satisfies both personal fulfillment and market demand.

Understanding your audience is critical. Each reader comes to your book with different expectations, whether seeking the emotional rollercoaster of friends-to-lovers dynamics or the heartwarming feel of a fake relationship turning real, as seen in *"The Unhoneymooners"* by Christina Lauren. Engage with your readers through social media or author events to understand their preferences. This direct line of communication can offer invaluable insights into the tropes and themes that capture their hearts, allowing you to tailor your stories to meet these desires while staying true to your creative vision.

Keep a finger on the pulse of market trends. While the allure of the billionaire alpha male or the bad boy with a heart of gold, as popularized by authors like J. Kenner and Jamie McGuire, may wax and wane, new trends are always on the horizon. For instance, the recent surge in popularity of grumpy-sunshine pairings offers a fresh take on opposites attract, highlighting how shifts in reader preferences can open new avenues for storytelling. Balancing these trends with your interests can help position your work in a sweet spot that appeals to a broad audience.

Don't shy away from experimentation. Writing across different sub-genres or mixing tropes can produce exciting discoveries about your strengths and reader preferences. Combining a slow-burn romance with a dash of comedy might reveal a talent for humor you hadn't tapped into, enriching your narrative toolkit. Each story you craft is a stepping stone towards defining your niche, an evolutionary and revolutionary process.

Once you've identified your niche, it's time to embrace it fully. Let's say you've discovered a knack for crafting spellbinding love stories set against the backdrop of small, quirky towns imbued with a sense of community and belonging. Lean into this discovery. Market your books by highlighting these elements that set your work apart, from the idyllic settings reminiscent of Jill Shalvis's *"Lucky Harbor"* series to the tight-knit relationships that echo the warmth of RaeAnne Thayne's *Haven Point*. Use tropes as anchors in your branding, signaling to readers exactly what they can expect from a book bearing your name.

Finding your niche involves a blend of self-awareness, genre exploration, audience engagement, market trend analysis, and creative experimentation. You can carve out a unique space in the genre by identifying the themes and tropes that resonate most strongly with you and your readers. Remember, your niche is not just where your book fits on a shelf—it's where your stories find a home in readers' hearts.

Chapter 32

Build a Strong Author Brand

Building a strong author brand is about much more than just a recognizable name or a consistent cover style. It's about creating a promise to your readers, a guarantee of the kind of emotional journey they can expect when they pick up one of your books. To establish a brand that resonates with contemporary romance readers, you need to start with a clear understanding of your voice as an author. Are you the architect of heartwarming tales that wrap the reader in a cozy blanket of warmth, akin to Debbie Macomber? Or do your stories sizzle with the intensity of a Sylvia Day novel? Identifying your unique voice and the themes you explore is the first step in crafting a brand that speaks to your target audience.

Once you've honed in on your authorial identity, it's time to communicate that brand effectively, and in today's digital age, an online presence is indispensable. A well-designed author website serves as the cornerstone of your digital marketing efforts, offering a hub where readers can learn more about you, your books, and any upcoming events or releases. Your website should reflect your brand's aesthetic and tone, whether that's through the use of romantic imagery for those who pen swoon-worthy tales or a sleek, minimalist design for authors of edgier romances. Including a blog or news section can also keep readers engaged, providing a behind-the-scenes look at your writing process or insights into your latest research adventures.

Social media platforms are another vital tool in building your author brand. Whether it's through X, Instagram, Facebook, or TikTok, each platform offers unique opportunities to connect with readers and share content that reflects your brand's personality. Instagram, with its visual focus, is perfect for sharing cover reveals, aesthetic inspiration boards, or snippets of your daily life that inspire your writing. X and Facebook can facilitate direct conversations with your readers, allowing you to engage in discussions, share updates, and promote your work in a more personal and interactive way. The key is consistency in your messaging and visuals across all platforms, reinforcing your brand identity at every touchpoint.

Content creation for social media should be strategic, aiming to entertain, inform, and engage your audience. Share writing tips, book recommendations, or personal anecdotes that align with your brand's voice. Utilize hash-tags to increase visibility and participate in genre-specific conversations to position yourself as an authority within the contemporary romance community. Running book give-aways, Q&A sessions, or live readings can also drive engagement and foster a sense of community among your readers.

Email marketing is another powerful strategy for building your author brand. By encouraging website visitors to sign up for your newsletter, you create a direct line of communication with your most engaged readers. Your newsletter can be a treasure trove of exclusive content, from sneak peeks of upcoming chapters to deep dives into your characters' back-stories. The personal nature of email allows you to cultivate a closer relationship with your readers, making them feel like part of an exclusive club—a tactic that can turn casual readers into loyal fans.

Building a strong author brand in contemporary romance isn't an overnight achievement; it's a continuous process that evolves with each book you publish and every interaction you have with your readers. By staying true to your voice, leveraging digital tools effectively, and engaging with your audience authentically, you can create a brand that not only stands out in the crowded romance market but also endears you to readers, ensuring they come back for every love story you have to tell. This strategic approach to branding and marketing is what transforms a writer into a beloved author whose books are eagerly anticipated and cherished.

Chapter 33

Cover Design and Titling

Cover design and titling in contemporary romance are not just about creating something that looks appealing; they are crucial elements that communicate the essence of your story to potential readers at first glance. A well-designed cover acts as a visual synopsis of the romance within, while an effective title serves as the hook that piques interest. Both elements must work harmoniously to promise readers the experience they seek in contemporary romance—be it a light-hearted rom-com, a steamy love affair, or a deep emotional journey. The cover and title are your first, and sometimes only, opportunity to grab a reader's attention in a crowded marketplace.

Current trends in cover design and titling often reflect broader cultural shifts and reader preferences. In contemporary romance, we're seeing a move towards bright, bold colors and minimalist designs that pop in thumbnail view—essential in the digital shopping environment. Illustrated covers have surged in popularity, particularly for romantic comedies and lighthearted romances, offering a charming and whimsical take that sets the tone before the first page is turned. Titles have become more playful and direct, often incorporating puns or familiar phrases that instantly convey the book's mood and genre. Keeping abreast of these trends is crucial, but so is ensuring that your cover and title remain authentic to your story's heart, avoiding the trap of blending into a sea of sameness.

Working with designers to create a visually appealing cover requires clear communication and trust. Start by conveying the mood, themes, and essential elements of your story. Sharing inspiration boards, favorite covers in your genre, and specific dos and don'ts can provide your designer with a solid foundation to begin their work. It's also important to discuss your target audience and any market trends you're keen to align with or avoid. Remember, a good designer brings not only their artistic skill but also their understanding of market trends and reader psychology to the table. Trusting their expertise, while ensuring they have a clear understanding of your vision, is key to a successful collaboration.

Feedback and revision are integral parts of the design process. Be open to your designer's ideas and suggestions, but don't shy away from requesting changes if the proposed design doesn't feel quite right. It can be helpful to test the cover options with a segment of your target audience, gathering insights that can inform the final design. Keep in mind that the goal is to create a cover that not only appeals to you and your designer but, more importantly, resonates with potential readers.

The title of your contemporary romance is another critical piece of the puzzle. A good title should not only be catchy and memorable but also reflective of the story's core. Work with your designer to ensure the typography matches the tone and theme of your book—elegant scripts for a swooning romance, bold and clean fonts for a modern love story. The title's placement, size, and color on the cover are also vital considerations, impacting legibility and attention in both physical and digital bookstore settings.

Staying true to the essence of your story in both cover design and titling cannot be overstated. While it's beneficial to be aware of trends, your cover and title should ultimately serve the story you've written. For instance, if your romance novel delves into deeper emotional themes, opting for a cover that's too whimsical might mislead readers, setting incorrect expectations. Similarly, a title that's too vague or abstract might fail to communicate the heart of your romance to potential readers.

The collaboration with your designer should be a creative partnership where both parties feel invested in the book's success. Prepare to discuss not just visual elements but the story itself—character dynamics, key scenes, or motifs that could inspire the design. This deeper understanding can lead to a cover that truly encapsulates the spirit of your romance.

Remember, the cover and title are often the final deciding factors for readers contemplating whether to give your book a chance. Investing the time and effort to get these elements right pays off in the long run, helping your book stand out in a crowded market and attract readers who are looking for exactly the kind of romance you've written.

Finally, consider the cover and title as part of your broader author brand. Consistency in style, typography, and thematic elements across your books can help readers quickly identify your work, building a visually cohesive brand that fans will recognize and trust. Whether you're a new author introducing your debut romance or an established writer with a loyal readership, the careful consideration of cover design and titling is crucial in captivating and retaining your audience.

The journey to a compelling cover and an effective title is a collaborative, creative process that demands attention to detail, an understanding of market trends, and, above all, a deep respect for the story you've crafted. By working closely with your designer and staying true to the essence of your romance, you can create a visual and verbal invitation that readers can't resist.

Epilogue

The contemporary romance market is a dynamic and ever-evolving landscape, offering a plethora of opportunities and challenges for authors. With its roots deeply embedded in the timeless desire for stories of love and connection, the genre has flourished, branching into a diverse array of subgenres that cater to a wide range of reader preferences. From the classic tales of star-crossed lovers to the modern narratives of digital dating, contemporary romance continues to captivate readers with its exploration of the complexities of the human heart. Understanding this market's depth and breadth is crucial for authors aiming to make their mark, requiring a keen awareness of both the traditional and emerging trends that shape reader expectations.

Publishing in contemporary romance offers various paths, each with its unique set of considerations. Traditional publishing, with its access to extensive distribution networks and marketing resources, remains a coveted route for many authors. However, the rise of self-publishing has democratized the field, allowing authors to take control of their publishing journey, from creative decisions to marketing and distribution. Hybrid models also exist, blending the best of both worlds, offering flexibility and broader opportunities for authors to reach their audiences. Navigating these options requires a clear understanding of one's career goals, resources, and the level of creative and financial control desired.

Reader expectations in contemporary romance are as diverse as the genre itself. Today's readers seek stories that not only provide escapism but also reflect the world's diversity and complexities. They crave authentic representations, emotional depth, and narratives that challenge traditional conventions of love and relationships. Meeting these expectations demands that authors remain attuned to the social and cultural shifts influencing reader preferences, ensuring their stories resonate on a personal and emotional level.

Building a sustainable writing career in contemporary romance goes beyond mastering the craft of storytelling. Networking plays a pivotal role, providing support, opportunities for collaboration, and insights into the publishing industry. Engaging with fellow authors, joining writing groups, and participating in literary events can open doors to valuable relationships and mentorships that enrich an author's career. These connections can offer encouragement during the challenges of the writing process and celebrate the milestones of success.

Continuing education is another cornerstone of a sustainable writing career. The landscape of contemporary romance and the publishing industry at large is continually changing, requiring authors to stay informed and adaptable. Workshops, courses, and conferences offer avenues for honing one's craft, learning about the latest market trends, and understanding the nuances of book marketing and promotion. This commitment to growth ensures that authors can evolve with the genre, maintaining the relevance and appeal of their work to readers.

Staying current with genre trends is essential for authors aiming to capture the interest of contemporary romance readers. This involves not just following the latest bestseller lists but also engaging with the romance reading community through social media, blogs, and book clubs. Listening to reader feedback, exploring new subgenres, and experimenting with emerging themes can inspire fresh and compelling narratives. However, while it's important to be aware of trends, authors should also strive to maintain their unique voice and perspective, offering stories that stand out in a crowded market.

In this digital footprint time period, an online presence is crucial for authors to connect with their audience, market their books, and build a personal brand. A strategic approach to social media, content marketing, and email newsletters can enhance visibility and foster a loyal readership. Authentic engagement with readers online, sharing behind-the-scenes glimpses of the writing process, and offering exclusive content can strengthen the reader-author bond, turning casual readers into dedicated fans.

Adapting to the changing landscape of contemporary romance requires resilience and a proactive mindset. The challenges of market saturation, shifting reader preferences, and the demands of self-promotion can be daunting. Yet, these challenges also present opportunities for innovation, collaboration, and personal growth. Authors who embrace these aspects of their career, continuously seeking to learn, evolve, and connect with their audience, are well-positioned to thrive in the contemporary romance market.

Ultimately, a sustainable writing career in contemporary romance is built on a foundation of passion, perseverance, and adaptability. It's about crafting stories that speak to the heart, engaging with the community that supports the genre, and remaining open to the lessons each step of the journey offers. By staying true to their voice, while also navigating the practicalities of the publishing industry and market trends, authors can not only achieve success but also contribute to the rich tapestry of contemporary romance, offering stories that entertain, inspire, and resonate with readers across the globe.

Thank You!

Thanks for making it to the end!

I hope you find this book helpful in your publishing journey.

We ask that you kindly leave a review!